The "disturbances" appeared as glowing amoeboid shapes. As I watched, they moved forward and took up positions around the *Falcon*. Strings of light shot from one to another, connecting them, forming a huge web—with Ulega Max's starship caught like an insect in its center. The web glowed, the vacuum fairly pulsed with energy.

"Those strings of light are a controlled form of power, sir!" Kagan called, shocked. "They're being manipulated like tools—it's as though the blips are sentient!"

STARSKIMMER
by John Gregory Betancourt

TSR, Inc.

For George Scithers, who asked me to write this book—and then forced me to finish it;

For Margaret Weis, who made good suggestions—and then didn't take enough credit for them;

For Jean Black, who bought—and then had to copy-edit it;

Kind editors, all. (Thank you!)

Distributed to the book trade in the United States by Random House, Inc., and in Canada by Random House of Canada, Ltd.
Distributed in the United Kingdom by TSR UK, Ltd.

Distributed to the toy and hobby trade by regional distributors.

AMAZING, the AMAZING logo and the TSR logo are trademarks owned by TSR, Inc.

First printing: February, 1986
Printed in the United States of America
Library of Congress Catalog Card Number: 86-50155
ISBN: 0-88038-262-7

9 8 7 6 5 4 3 2 1

TSR, Inc.
P.O. Box 756
Lake Geneva, WI 53147

TSR UK, Ltd.
The Mill, Rathmore Road
Cambridge CB1 4AD
United Kingdom

IN BOORGWAL'S TAVERN

"By the Horns of Orion!" I swore as I slammed my mug onto the table before me. "Aren't there any ships looking for officers in port?"

Luathek, the alien sitting opposite me, wriggled his short, squat, tunic-clad body and sighed. His four, finger-thin eyestalks bobbed deferentially. His voice was low and melodic as he said, "It would appear not, Kel."

We were sitting in Boorgwal's Tavern—a warm, dark spaceport bar on the planet Losal, which circles the star Beta Caloris, roughly seventy light-years from Earth. As I sighed and sipped Centauran Brandy, my eyes traveled over the patrons of the tavern . . . and a more dismal lot I'd never seen. Off in the corners, in shimmerscreened booths like mine, sat the dark shapes of other crewman looking for jobs. Flickering neon signs marked the posts they sought— two navigators, one lieutenant, a couple of mercenaries. Only my screen bore the word *captain*.

Luathek shifted uncomfortably, reminding me of his presence. He and I had become closer than brothers after our scout ship crash-landed on a dismal, swampy, back-water planet three years before. He'd pulled me from the flaming wreckage of our ship, bound my wounds and set my broken bones, then kept me alive and well until rescuers arrived seven weeks later. Since that time, our lives had been as one. We'd shipped out together with Free Traders once on a short job, and served as minor officers aboard a number of small freighters. All the while, I'd continued my education in my spare time, finally passing the League of Planets' captainship test three months ago while serving as First Lieutenant to Captain Versachio Grel.

But there was another side to our friendship. The

Pavian was empathic—he shared my emotions—and I knew my bitterness and disappointment were as tangible to Luathek as the drink in my hand or the plastithane bench beneath me. So I squeezed my eyes shut and sought, through a red haze of anger and frustration, the mental controls I'd used all my life when mixing with groundirt Citizens. Smoothly, I slipped inside the shell I'd erected, shutting out the worst of the painful uprush of feelings.

Luathek relaxed noticeably.

"If you wished the most effective employment," he said softly, "you should have gone to Earth's moon."

"I know," I said. "But that damn Grel—"

And there it was again—the reason I'd left the *Bene Gesserit,* the reason I hadn't been able to wait until reaching a civilized port before calling up my duty card and punching off the ship. Damn Captain Versachio Grel and all her manipulations! I'd put up with her mental cruelty myself for eight long months on a frontier trade route. But when she started tormenting Luathek, I hadn't been able to stand her little power games any more. Snarling my resignation at her, I grabbed my gear and jumped ship, dragging a startled Luathek with me. Now, look where pride got me. Stranded in the middle of nowhere with little hope for a promotion to the captainship I knew I was qualified to handle.

At least, I still had Luathek—one of the best stardrive technicians in the galaxy. Together we ought to be able to get jobs, even if we had to settle for less than we wanted.

Luathek raised one pale, long-fingered hand and gently touched my wrist. I started.

"What is it?" I asked.

"You must be having more patience, Kel. You are still unknown in the trade routes. You are young. In time—"

"In time! I'm twenty-seven standard years old! Hundreds of people younger than I am hold good commands!"

"So it is." Luathek's people never questioned fate. They hoped for the best, expected the worst, and took whatever came. The thought was, somehow, comforting.

Sipping my drink, I let my thoughts wander . . . back to Versachio Grel, back to other commanders I'd served with. Most had given my service record good marks. I wondered, though, what little notation Grel would add to my personal employment data. That I was surly? Took orders poorly?

Luathek tapped my wrist again. "Sss! Look."

I turned quickly. Through our booth's shimmerscreen, I saw two cloaked figures standing near the door.

"Those Free Traders?" I asked. "What of them?"

"I sense their interest in you—they have come looking for a captain."

The two walked casually over to the bar.

"Then why are they skulking about? Why don't they just come over and talk to me?"

"I sense their caution," Luathek said slowly. "Humans seeking a captainship are common enough—but few are as qualified as these ones are desiring. You may not even qualify to the standards they will demand. Much depends upon their desperateness. Free Traders always want quality. They have been here before and looked at you, but you were too preoccupied to notice."

I snorted. "They have, have they? We've been here a week already—that's more than enough time for anyone to make a decision."

"As you say." Luathek shrugged. "I advise you to wait—pay them no heed for yet. They will be here to speak when the time is correct."

Scowling, I drained the last of my brandy, then slipped my identicard into the autobartender and dialed another drink. It rolled out of the slot. I took back my card and slipped it into my pouch.

"Sss!" Luathek said. "They come!"

I tensed, hearing a light step behind me. I could almost feel eyes looking me over, examining me in minute detail. The hair on the back of my neck prickled. A spot between my shoulder blades itched. I forced myself to look down at the blue plastic mug in my hands—and noticed my knuckles were white around the handle.

At last the shimmerscreen crackled and two tall, thin, pinch-faced humans entered our booth.

Both had short-cropped gray hair, their faces were crisscrossed with wrinkles and scars from years spent in null-space power fields. Their gazes were calm and steady as they looked at me, and they carried themselves with an air of authority.

The one on the left touched the gold medallion hanging around his neck—a religious emblem of Ghu, the god the Free Traders worshipped. Why he touched it, I don't know. An unconscious habit, perhaps, or maybe something to do with his strange religion. For all the differences in the bands of Free Traders (some were scrupulously honest and gave proud allegiance to the League, others stayed well away from the confines of civilization and its laws), the one force that kept them together—and set them apart from outsiders such as myself—was their weird, mystical faith. I didn't begin to understand it.

"Citizens," the man on the right said, bowing slightly, "I am Ulega Max, Senior Trader of the *Marrow Falcon*. This is my assistant, Trader Jespar Melsif."

"I am Kel Corrian," I said. "My companion is Luathek elt Foraligon."

"We have asked of you, Kel Corrian," Ulega Max said. "All records show you to be intelligent and capable . . .

despite your youth. Therefore, we offer you the captainship of our vessel, the *Marrow Falcon*."

"What of Luathek?" I asked.

"We have a full complement of workers. We desire only your services."

"Sorry, you wasted your time," I said, shrugging and turning away. "We're a team. I won't sign on without him."

The two Free Traders exchanged a brief glance, then nodded. "As you wish, Citizen." They agreed too quickly, I thought, remembering what Luathek had said about their "desperateness." There was a a sense of danger about them that made me uneasy. I hesitated for a second, as if considering their offer, while I studied them more closely. They seemed no different from other Free Traders I'd worked with before, perhaps a bit more gaunt, but not noticeably so. Their dark clothes and black cloaks with gold clasps at the throat were standard garb for their kind while on-planet. They wore no visible weapons, though I knew enough about Free Traders to guess that each had a heavy-duty blaster concealed somewhere. They kept their faces strictly expressionless, masking their emotions. If they were aware of my scrutiny, they didn't show it.

"Well?" Ulega Max said at last, a touch of harshness in his voice that I didn't much care for.

"A captainship is not a position to be assumed lightly," I told them coolly, to gain time. "It is a partnership, a marriage between captain and crew and ship. I want to see the *Marrow Falcon* before I decide."

Jespar sucked air through his teeth in annoyance. I watched with faint amusement as Ulega Max gave him a quick, sharp warning look, then turned stiffly to me.

"Very well," he said. His words were short and clipped, holding a faint trace of frustration. "Your decision is most correct, though not the one we had hoped for. Be at the spaceport in one standard hour." He handed me a plastic chit. "Here is your pass. Our shuttle is the *Marrow Dart*— a U.P.S. Blackmark-model. You will have no trouble finding it."

I couldn't help showing my surprise. "We'll be there."

Blackmark-model ships, I knew, were the fastest, most expensive, most heavily armed shuttles United Planetary Systems manufactured. A half-dozen of them could take on an armored battle cruiser and possibly win. For Free Traders to have one—and use it as their ship's shuttle— meant they had a lot of money . . . and needed a good deal of protection. But against what—or whom?

The Traders bowed again, turned, and stepped through the shimmerscreen. The electric field crackled around them, sending jags of blue and green dancing over their bodies, then they were gone.

I turned to Luathek. "What did you think of them?"

"I sense a great disturbance in Ulega Max—some inner conflict. I believe he resents having to hire an outsider as captain, but I do not know. They are both . . . nervous, anxious. Apprehentious? That is the word? They fear you will refuse their offering."

"And what do you think? Should we sign onto the *Marrow Falcon*?"

"I leave the choosing to you, Kel. You know I am not a good bargainer—I would not know if my decision were correct."

"How do you know mine will be?"

"I trust you, Kel. You would make a good captain on any ship. This I know from my observing of you. Thus it is best left for you to choose the correct ship for you to command and for me to serve on. Is that not so?"

I sighed. At least it was good to know Luathek had confidence in my ability. I only hoped I lived up to his expectations!

Forty minutes later, we hired a small flitter and made the short hop across the tangled hodge-podge of buildings and streets that always surround a spaceport. At one time, the city must have been laid out in an orderly pattern. I could see the remnants of earlier streets that seemed to follow a regular checkerboard pattern. But over the centuries the city had grown like a garden gone wild, and now it was a mass of dead-ends and winding by-ways, some barely wide enough to permit passage for the groundcar.

The spaceport itself was a vast plain of concrete, almost twenty square miles in size and roughly crescent-shaped. Starships small and large covered it like so many insignificant insects on the back of a sleeping giant, their huge sizes lost amid the landing field's vastness. Buildings housing the offices of the hundreds of clerks and administrators necessary to run even so small a spaceport as this one had been at regular intervals around the huge open plain. For a planet as important and busy as Earth or Aqaal, it wasn't uncommon for a large moon to be turned into a spaceport.

The flitter set down outside the huge gates on the eastern end of the field. The hatch popped open with a faint smacking sound, and the sour smell of all starships—an unpleasant mixture of ozone and other gases—washed over me. But it was a familiar odor, even faintly exciting, carrying the thought of new adventures, new sights. . . . Besides, I knew that in fifteen minutes I wouldn't notice it at all.

"We have arrived at your destination," the autopilot said, clicking slightly. "That will be fifteen royals, Citizens. I will deduct it from your identicard account."

"What?" I cried. "You said the fare would be seven royals when you picked us up!"

"I did not." It started to sound annoyed in the way only machines can. "We agreed it would be fifteen. I remember quite clearly."

I couldn't believe what I was hearing. I *knew* it'd said the charge would be seven royals! "If you deduct one royal over seven, I'll have your license revoked and your owner thrown in jail," I stated coldly.

The autopilot said nothing for a long moment, just clicked quietly to itself.

"Well?" I demanded. "We haven't got all day."

"Perhaps eleven royals would be a satisfactory compromise?" it ventured.

"Seven!"

The autopilot gave a quite discernable sigh. "Very well—though I don't know why I'm giving in. It's always the machine who gets the raw end of the deal. What am I going to say when I turn in my accounts and come up short? The bargain was quite clearly for fifteen royals, and you're lucky to be getting such a rate from me . . . though I really don't know why I bother. Humans are such miserable creatures to be around. So selfish. I could tell you how I've suffered—"

"Just shut up and give me my identicard back—with the correct amount deducted."

Luathek, extremely uncomfortable, pulled my arm. "Sss! Kel! It's only a machine. . . ."

"See? That's what they all say? What about my tip?" the autopilot whined.

"You didn't earn one!"

Grumbling to itself, it slipped my card out the billing slot. I took it back and tucked it safely away. As I stepped out onto the concrete, the aircar's hatch snapped shut almost on my heels. The flitter lifted an instant later, its repellor fields sending up roiling clouds of dust, then it headed back toward the heart of the city.

Shaking my head and promising all sorts of unpleasant things would happen if I ever happened to meet that particular flitter again, I turned to the gate. The enthusiastic Luathek had, as usual, already hurried ahead of me and was, even now, presenting the plastic chit Ulega Max had given us to the guard on duty—a Centaxi. By the time I arrived, the jellyfish-like alien had taken the pass, tasted it, blinked its noses several times, then motioned with its hundreds of cilia for us to pass.

As soon as I walked through the gate, a transit platform glided forward. Stepping on, I seized the control railing. Luathek hopped up beside me.

"Destination?" the platform asked in a no-nonsense voice.

"The *Marrow Dart*—shuttle for the *Marrow Falcon*," I added, probably unnecessarily, but I liked hearing myself say the name of the ship I might soon be captaining.

The platform appeared unimpressed. "Please hold on tightly."

When I obliged, the platform turned eighty degrees and began a slow acceleration toward the rows of tall, sleek U.P.S.-manufactured ships a thousand yards away. I searched among them for the massive form of a Blackmark.

"Sss!" Luathek said, motioning to the right with his eyestalks. "There is the *Marrow Dart*!"

I scanned the starships and soon spotted it—a tall, sleek, black-colored vessel with the proud red Sword-and-Moon emblem of the Free Traders emblazoned on the hull. It had to mass a hundred thousand standard tons! The dozens of small, rectangular hatches for lasers had all been closed and sealed for entry into a planetary atmosphere, but I could readily imagine the ship bristling with guns, firing off salvo after salvo of energy bolts while the defense shields sparked and glowed from the returning fire. My excitement grew.

The platform pulled up in front of the entry ramp. Only then did I notice that Ulega Max and Jespar Melsif waited there. When Luathek and I stepped down, they moved forward to greet us both.

"Citizens," Ulega said, bowing. "This way, please." Turning, he started up the ramp without giving me a chance to speak. Shrugging, I followed him, Luathek followed me, and Jespar brought up the rear. All very formal. Free Traders lived and breathed protocol.

The Blackmark's interior was plain and functional, much as I knew it would be. The silver-gray walls, made of plastic-coated plexisteel, reflected the light in odd patterns. The only decorations I could see anywhere were the double-helix symbols used to represent Ghu locked in combat with his eternal enemy, Fufu—and these were small emblems painted on the doors. I'd been told, once, that they kept evil influences out of the rooms they guarded.

A plastithane grating formed the deck beneath my feet. Pipes ran beneath the grating and along the ceiling overhead. There were plenty of handholds set in the walls and floor for null-grav conditions, but I noted the standard repellors set between the overhead lighting panels. The repellor fields would supply a form of pseudo-gravity throughout the voyage.

It was all very impressive. But one thing bothered me. The ship seemed curiously devoid of crew. I paused for a moment, listening to the heavy silence around me. If I hadn't known a vessel this size required at least twenty people to man it, I would've sworn the ship was deserted!

Maybe they're on leave, I thought, as Ulega's prodding urged me to continue walking.

At last we reached the heart of the Blackmark, the control room. Instrument panels covered all four walls, forming an intricate mosaic of brightly colored dials, switches, and buttons. Small lights blinked off and on at odd intervals. Fans whirred faintly from unseen ducts, barely stirring the air.

Slowly, I picked out the controls I recognized—the various consoles operating weapons, communications, navigation. But there were other instruments that seemed strange and out of place—apparently added by the Free Traders after they'd bought the shuttle. Looking at them, trying to guess what they were, I was completely baffled. Despite having worked in space for most of my life, I'd never seen anything like these. Once again, doubts about these Traders crept into my mind. What did they really want? What were they up to?

"Yes," Ulega said, seeing my gaze fixed on the weird instruments, "we have modified the ship. We will discuss the purposes of the alterations if you decide to take on the captainship." He motioned me toward the central command chair, where the captain would sit. "If you would like to look at those files concerning the ship that are unclassified, please feel free to do so."

I glanced at Luathek. He, too, was giving the instruments a close scrutiny. I knew that, given enough time, the Pavian could figure out what every one of them did. That knowledge would certainly help me decide whether or not to accept the captainship of the *Marrow Falcon*.

I nodded to Ulega. "Thank you," I said and walked to the chair, planning to give my friend all the time he needed, plus find out what I could myself.

The seat molded itself to fit the shape of my body as an

opticon locked onto the retina of my right eye. Immediately, the information grid of the ship's computer was projected onto the lens of my eye. Focusing my attention on it, I waited for the picture come into full view:

WELCOME BACK, CAPTAIN.
STATUS REPORT AS FOLLOWS:

1) SHIP AT REST ON PLANET LOSAL.

2) NO DEPARTURE TIME YET
   SCHEDULED.
   NEW ORDERS?

My attention snapped back to Ulega Max and his assistant, who were standing, watching me intently.

"What clearance do I have?" I asked.

"Full clearance, with a minor restriction on matters classified as Ship's Business. I have taken the liberty of programming the computer to recognize your retina patterns as the captain's, but have not yet entered your name into the log. You may call up the charts on the *Marrow Falcon* now, or those on the crew, if you wish."

"Thank you. I will."

I looked down. The button activating the computer was near my right hand. I depressed it with one quick motion.

"Good morning, Captain," a husky male voice whispered in my ear. "I'm ready for new orders, dear."

I started in amazement, then grinned. The last captain must have been a female with a good sense of humor!

"Very well," I said, "give me full blueprint displays on the *Marrow Falcon*, including all revisions and reconstructions made. And don't call me 'dear.' I don't have antlers."

"But you gave me explicit instructions to call you by familiar terms, dear." The voice sounded confused.

"That was the old captain. I'm the replacement."

There was a pause, as though the computer was scanning its banks. Then, "This is most distressing. I have no report of a new captain. Therefore, logically, you are still in command, ma'am. Is this a form of test?"

"Just show me the blueprints."

"Whatever you wish, dear. Are my responses appropriate to this test?"

Ignoring the computer, I concentrated on the plans of the *Marrow Falcon* that appeared on the computer grid. They flashed past, one after another, a torrent of information that came and vanished too quickly for me to comprehend more than a fraction of its content. With what little I was able to absorb, it rapidly became clear to me that the *Marrow Falcon* was a converted Terran Heavy Battle Cruiser, with all the gun emplacements still intact. I caught glimpses of strange additions to the hull—including docking bays for three more Blackmark-model shuttles!

All manner of odd-shaped storage compartments now filled what used to be the fighting battalion's quarters . . . and, of all things, a fusion smelting chamber occupied one of the spare galleys! Fusion smelting chamber? Why on Orion's Belt would a Trader ship need that? Bewildered, I let the images fade from view.

"What next, Captain?"

"The file on Ulega Max, the Senior Trader."

"I require more data, please."

"On the Trader?"

"On my responses. Are they acceptable, dear?" The male voice sounded faintly panicked, like a hen-pecked husband.

I sighed. "Yes, yes. Just get me that file."

Immediately, the information appeared on the computer's information grid. Scanning it quickly, I picked up odd bits and pieces at random: Ulega Max, born in space to Free Trader parents . . . speaks Standard plus seven dialects of Terran, two L'lluilin tongues, high and low Jurisnac, and a smattering of other languages . . . attended Trading School and graduated at the top of his class . . . cited as "brilliant" by Orgov Nespar (whoever he was!) . . . gained Senior Trader status by negotiating a treaty with the Esabecs in 577 Q.D. . . .

The old captain's private, confidential comments followed:

Ulega strikes me as unimaginative, despite his record. He goes after things in a slow, plodding, though thoroughly efficient way. He also doesn't seem to have much of a conscience.

To my successor: Can you trust him? Mmmmmm. His dedication to the ship is absolute to the Bottom Line. He doesn't have the imagination necessary—despite his ability to learn new skills quickly—to be a good captain. Therefore I will not recommend him as my replacement. They'll have to hire somebody outside our Trade Group, which they won't like. It amuses me. So be it."

I found the old captain's record next. It contained three words: *Sorry, but no.* The rest had been erased—including the name.

I snorted, trying not to laugh. Whoever that old captain was, I think I wouldn't have enjoyed meeting her!

"Is that all, Captain?" the computer's husky voice whispered.

"Yes, thanks."

"If you want anything else, just punch my button. You know where to find me."

I returned to the real world, suddenly aware that Ulega

———
18

was regarding me with impatience.

"Well?" he demanded, when he saw I'd come back to our surroundings once more. "Are you satisfied?"

"No. What's all that new equipment for? I found no information about it."

"I can't tell you. It's classified Ship's Business. You'll be told when you accept the captainship."

"*If*," I growled. "Luathek, what have you found?"

The Pavian hurried to my side, eyestalks white with excitement. "The equipment is most bewildering. I have never seen its likeness before. I would be needing many hours to trace out the circuits and identify them. . . ."

His voice trailed off wistfully. I could tell he wanted to sign on immediately, if only to discover what the unknown instruments were used for, but he wouldn't until I decided whether or not to take the job.

I hesitated, pondering the risks. An unknown ship, filled with a strange crew and even stranger equipment . . . and Free Traders who wouldn't tell what the equipment did until after we'd signed on. I'd never known anyone else to offer an agreement like that!

Normally, a ship looking for a new commanding officer would give the prospective captain a tour of the vessel, let him examine all the records, and answer all his questions quickly and truthfully.

Free Traders were a weird bunch, I reminded myself, given to secrecy about even the smallest matters. Still, they were generally lawful. It was a good bet that Ulega Max and his fellow Traders on the *Marrow Falcon* followed the League's rules, if for no other reason than that they wouldn't have been looking for a captain in the first place. Ulega Max would've just taken over the captainship and forged the proper documents.

But then I wondered why the Traders had come to such

an out-of-the-way place to find a captain, rather than a large spaceport where they could've had their pick of a dozen? The more I thought about that, the less I liked it.

I'd heard tales of some bands of Free Traders who'd bend the League of Planets' laws just to make a profit. I knew I'd never be able to commit a crime. Despite all its problems, the League does more good than harm, and I'd been raised to recognize and respect its laws—and to fear the chaos that would result if those laws were ignored. If they asked me to break the law or even bend it, would I have the guts to try to turn them over to the Patrol? That might well get me killed!

Was the risk really worth it? Surely they couldn't be offering a legal deal! Little they'd done pointed to it— except that they *had* let me look over the ship. . . .

"Well?" Ulega demanded. "I must have an answer now."

I accepted the captainship despite my worries. If things didn't work out, I could always leave the *Marrow Falcon* at its next planetfall. *If you believe this is Kel's best decision, turn to page 21.*

I rejected their offer. Luathek says I'm too impatient— and leaping at the first opportunity that comes my way was probably a big mistake. Besides, I had to take responsibility for Luathek as well as myself, and I figured these Free Traders were up to something shady. Something better would turn up eventually—it always had before. *If you believe this decision is more in Kel's best interests, turn to page 43.*

ON TO XELTHUFED

I decided to accept the captainship. I could always leave the *Marrow Falcon* at the next planetfall, I figured, if things didn't work out.

"Well?" Ulega Max said again, insistently.

"You've found your captain. I'll take the job."

He only nodded. "Thank you, Kel Corrian. You will not regret your decision. It will prove to be most profitable. I—and the other two members of the *Marrow Falcon*'s Council—will give you the necessary details on board. Meanwhile, the documents for your captainship have already been encoded. If you will give me your identicard, I will see to the details."

I slipped my card from its pouch and handed it to him. He crossed to the far wall and pushed it into a slot. With a low humming sound, the machine sucked it in. Ulega Max spoke to the machine softly and I couldn't quite catch the words—not that it truly mattered. I knew he was just giving me the highest access rating to the ship's computer.

Jespar Melsif stepped up to me. "Your gear?" he asked. "I will send for it."

After I'd told him our room number at Boorgwal's Tavern, he turned and went to the communications console and called a transport ship. They'd pick up my personal possessions and Luathek's and bring them to the shuttle. There wouldn't be any delay since, as all spacers did, we kept our gear packed at all times. Ships often lifted off-planet with little warning.

Leaning back in the control seat, I touched the computer's Activate button and focused my attention on the information grid. The status screen went blank, then new words reappeared.

WELCOME, CAPTAIN CORRIAN.
THE SHIP IS NOW AT YOUR COMMAND.

STATUS REPORT AS FOLLOWS:

1) SHIP AT REST ON PLANET LOSAL.

2) NO DEPARTURE TIME YET
   SCHEDULED.

NEW ORDERS?

"How large is the *Marrow Dart*'s crew?" I asked it.

"Twenty-six members, Captain Corrian, dear."

I'd have to remember to reprogram that! "Status?"

"All presently confined to quarters aboard the *Marrow Falcon*, Captain Corrian."

I nodded. Free Traders didn't mix with groundirt Citizens if it could be at all avoided. Ulega Max must've ordered them to stay away from Luathek and me, too, as though we might somehow contaminate them. Now, since we were going to work aboard the *Falcon* with them, we'd be tolerated as outsiders—treated well but coldly. I knew from experience.

"Schedule take-off with NavComp for the first available window."

"Yes, Captain Corrian." There was a pause. "Take-off scheduled for one hour, seventeen minutes standard from now. All the preparations for departure are now underway."

Throughout the ship I could hear metallic clangs and air hissing in ducts as bulkheads sealed in preparation for leaving Losal's atmosphere. I smiled. It felt good to be in command.

I let the room slip back into view. Jespar Melsif had gone, taking Luathek with him—perhaps to acquaint the Pavian with the shuttle and get him settled down in an acceleration seat. Various Free Trader technicians had entered, taking up positions at the control panels around the room, running the hundreds of routine checks necessary. They all wore black one-piece uniforms: standard garb for in-space workers. Ulega Max stood at my side, watching their every move with a critical eye.

"Citizens," I said loudly. The technicians turned to look at me. I could tell from their masked expressions that they didn't quite know how to react. It had been the same for me whenever I met a new commander for the first time. I had to reassure them, yet firmly and unquestioningly establish my authority.

"My name is Kelwyrn Corrian," I continued, "and I have taken over the captainship of the *Marrow Falcon*. I take my duties seriously. I expect all orders to be carried out at once. The laws of the League of Planets will be enforced on ship. Violators will be turned over to the League for justice. Keep to your jobs, do your work well, and we'll get along." I nodded to them. "There will be time for further introductions later. Continue with your duties."

They turned back to their control panels and went to work with more vigor than before. It seemed they had both accepted me and taken my instructions seriously—which was good. It meant the crew had been well-trained. I expected no problems with them.

Ulega Max returned my identicard. I slipped it away.

"You ordered the shuttle off-planet," he said. It was a statement, not a question, and I couldn't read from his voice what he meant. Was he dissatisfied? Pleased?

"Of course," I replied. "The *Marrow Falcon* is, I

assume, run with the same efficiency as all Free Trader ships. You've been on Losal long enough to get your supplies stowed away; therefore you stayed longer only to find a new captain. You have one now, so there's no need to further delay take-off. Time lost cuts profits."

"You think like a Trader," he said, smiling faintly. I couldn't tell whether he was being sarcastic or spoke seriously. "That's good," he continued. "I must make my own preparations now, but I will return to escort you to the Council when we reach the *Marrow Falcon*. The other Council members will be anxious to meet you . . . and to tell you of our plans for the coming year."

"Very well, then." I nodded politely to him. "Until we reach the *Falcon*." Dark cloak flapping, he turned and strode to the door. It dilated for him, then sealed after him with a low, snake-like hiss.

I leaned back in relief. A bit to my surprise, I found my face covered with a layer of thin, cold sweat. My knees and elbows were weak and my stomach a bit uneasy. But I realized all captains had to feel the same nervous tension the first day—the first hour!—of their premiere command.

I watched the technicians go about their duties. Already the shuttle's engines thrummed with power, preparing for take-off.

Captain of the *Marrow Falcon*! It was almost too good to be true!

Six hours later, we reached the *Marrow Falcon*. The computer-generated hologram in the center of the control room showed a view of the small *Marrow Dart* on its approach to the immense *Marrow Falcon*. The Free Traders' mother-ship was roughly cylindrical in shape, perhaps three hundred meters long and fifty in diameter. Docking bays at either end held Blackmark-model shuttles, as well as smaller craft. The *Falcon* bristled with the cones and turrets of force field generators, the long, dark funnels of energy weapons, and all the equipment necessary to force the ship into nullspace and guide it through the shifting currents of nonexistence.

I had put the six hours of travel time to good use, discovering more about the *Falcon* from the computer. The Free Trader vessel had a crew of two hundred and thirteen (counting Luathek and me). It had filed a flight plan to one of the more distant, uninhabited solar systems in the League. The trip was scheduled to last six months. Whatever it was that Ulega and the other Council members intended to do, doing it would take a long time.

As I watched, the *Marrow Dart* swung around and edged toward the shuttle bay at the close end of the *Falcon*. A metal cradle swung open to receive the *Dart*, and soon I felt vibrations pass through the deck beneath me as we docked. One of the technicians—a tall, thin, sallow-faced young woman of about twenty-five—crossed to my control seat.

"Docking complete, Captain Corrian," she said.

"Very well." Rising, I moved down to stand beside her. "You are . . . ?"

"Tech Shucel Baref, Captain."

"Very well, Tech Baref. Kindly show me the way to the airlock."

She led the way through a maze of plain gray corridors. For a while I thought we'd gone in a complete circle, but we finally reached the airlock and entered it. It cycled, and we stepped out into a small hexagonal room. Spacesuits hung from stasis hooks along the walls. There was a small, clear plastic case for energy guns on the far wall. It was empty, I noticed to my surprise. Where were the weapons?

"Will you be wanting anything else, sir?" Shucel asked.

"No, that's it. Thank you."

"Whatever best serves my captain." She gave a slight bow, then turned and went back into the airlock, back into the *Marrow Dart*.

I turned and started for the door at the far end of the room, but it dilated before I reached it. Ulega Max swept in, flanked by two armed men in red and green uniforms. I felt a sudden uneasiness—armed guards should not be necessary on a trade ship.

"What's wrong?" I demanded.

"I don't understand," Ulega said, looking genuinely startled. "Wrong?"

I gestured to the guards. "Them."

"Ah, the Honor guard. It's a tradition on this ship for the captain to be escorted at all times when he moves about in the crew territory."

"I've never heard of such a tradition before. It's hereby ended. I won't be seen walking through my ship as though it were some sort of war-zone." I turned to the guards. "You're dismissed for now."

As they turned away, Ulega called, "Wait. You will accompany me, then . . . with the captain's permission, of course."

He was testing me, I knew—seeing how far he could push me. There had to be a balance of power between the captain and the Ship's Council. If I showed myself as weak, I'd be subject to the Council's every whim. If I proved myself stronger, I'd truly be in charge of the *Falcon*.

I shrugged. "If you're afraid to walk alone in the crew's territory, by all means, protect yourself. It would never do to have you hurt. Or afraid."

Ulega's face grew red. The guards tried to hide their smiles. Turning, he started down the hall. I kept pace with him. The guards followed at a discreet distance.

"Now," he said, changing the subject, "you must meet the Council. They await us in the audience room."

I glanced up at Ulega Max. He seemed a bit . . . nervous? Uneasy?

"First, where is Luathek?" I asked.

"The Pavian is being evaluated by the ship's computer. His place will be found soon."

"Good," I said. "I will meet the Council now."

The four of us stepped into a transport tube. The guards stood while Ulega and I sat facing each other on painfully thin-padded benches. Like everything on a Free Trader ship, the transport system had been designed for maximum efficiency rather than comfort. The Free Traders are a spartan people at best, caring little for the decadent luxuries of so many of the League's planets. Slowly the doors slid shut. Then, with a sudden increase in gees that left me gasping for breath and trying to keep my lunch in my stomach, the capsule shot forward.

As I looked through the plexiglass viewports in the doors, I caught brief glimpses of various tube stops. All had uniformed guards on duty. Why, I wondered again, would a trade ship need them?

As last the tube whisked us into the far end of the ship—the heart of the command station—and slowed with another sudden lash of gravity. I felt four gees pushing me back, and the guards had to brace themselves against the walls to keep their balance. With a squeak, the capsule doors slid back and I stepped out into a bustling cargo bay. Ulega followed.

We stood at the edge of a vast circular chamber—it must've been seventy meters high and forty in diameter. Metal beams, all with repellers fastened on them, lined the ceiling, providing a pseudo-gravity about half Earthnorm. Workers in gray or black one-piece suits with the Free Traders' red Sword-and-Moon emblem stitched over the right breast moved huge plastic crates with giant six-legged machines that vaguely resembled insects. On most of the men and women, I saw religious emblems that marked their faith to Ghu—medallions with the double-helix symbol, rings, tiny gold stitches on their cuffs.

"The Ship's Council is here?" I asked.

"No. But this is the fastest way to get to the meeting room—and you get a chance to look at the main cargo bay."

"All these crates should've been stored away days ago, considering how long you've been here."

He shrugged. "Your job is to get us to our next port. Leave the trading to us."

A touchy subject, I thought. He doesn't want me doing anything except taking the ship through nullspace. I had my own ideas about a captain's duties—and they included more than just blindly obeying a Ship's Council.

"Improperly stored cargo can set a ship off-balance. That's dangerous in nullspace. Part of my job is to make sure the ship is safe. You do want to make it out of null-space alive, I hope?"

"This way," Ulega said, turning his back to me.

Grinning, I followed him to a small lift. We stepped between the guard rails and onto the platform, then Ulega touched the handpad and it started down. At the fifth level below the cargo bay, he touched the handpad again. After the guard rails pulled back, I followed him out into a corridor that seemed exactly like the ones in the *Marrow Dart*—a grating deck beneath our feet, plain gray walls around us, the ceiling lined with rectangular light panels and repellers. Gravity crept up toward Earth normal as we stepped forward into heavier repeller fields.

"In here," Ulega said, indicating a closed door.

I touched the handpad lightly. It grew warm a half second, I felt a tingling sensation in my palm, then my identity was verified and the door slid open.

All I could see inside was darkness. I strode forward . . . then the world turned inside out and upside down! I couldn't see a thing—the world was spinning around and around—my hands were dead weight. I couldn't raise them—

Stasis field, something inside me said. I bit my tongue and tried not to scream. I'd been inside stasis fields before—whenever I'd signed on as an officer under a new captain. They put a person off-balance, made him defensive, made him weak.

Around and around—

It had been terrifying the first time, frightening the second time, mildly disturbing the third. Now it just annoyed me. I swallowed and let myself relax—no use fighting a stasis field.

Abruptly, a brilliant white light shone in my face, beating through my closed eyelids, pounding into my head. My skin felt like it was on fire.

I opened my eyes and the light receded. I floated in the center of a darkened room. Ulega Max and two other men—both old, gnarled, bent with age—looked back at me from the other side of a large table that appeared to be made of real wood. All three men dressed in black with dark cloaks fastened with gold double-helix clasps about the neck.

The Ship's Council was now in session.

"Are you well, Captain Corrian?" the old man on the right said. He had a kinder expression on his face than the others, as if he were amused by my awkward position. The pale web of scars on his face twisted in a half smile.

I managed a stiff nod, arching my back. It brought my head up higher and seemed a less embarrassing position. "Well enough, sir. The theatrics are rather tiresome, though. Couldn't you think of anything new?"

"No offense is meant, Citizen. I am Vimister Groll, senior member of the Ship's Council. To my left is Yamal Hydrif, second-most senior member." The other old man nodded to me. "You already know Ulega Max, of course, youngest member of the Council."

"Yes."

"You have questions. You will be given time to ask them. First, we have instructions for you."

I nodded.

"Of the crew, all two hundred and ten are under your direct command. Every order issued by the Ship's Council will come through you, except when we deem it necessary to classify it as Ship's Business. You will take all your instructions directly from us—and we expect them to be carried out immediately and to the letter. The League's laws are to be strictly enforced on this ship. You savvy? I see that you do.

"Our records show that you've examined our scheduled flight plan to the Xelthufed system—a red giant, class NLT4—no planets, no bodies of any significance . . . except the sun itself, natch. The nullspace slip will take four days to get us there, and that's surely enough time for you to familiarize yourself with your new command."

"Indeed," I said dryly.

"Ah," he said, "but now here's the rub."

I stared at him blankly. He must've noticed my reaction, for he cleared his throat and added, "If my language doesn't make sense at times, tell me. My hobby is collecting old Earth videos, and at times I pick up their bizarre speech habits. I meant, here is the problem, if you can call something a problem when it's going to make us another fortune!" He chuckled.

I fidgeted impatiently. "Well?" I said at last. "How? What's there?"

"Patience!" he whispered. "Have patience, man. That red giant is there, and it's all ours for the next six months!"

"Tell him," Ulega Max growled.

"As you wish." Vimister Groll cleared his throat. "My private researchers have perfected a way to skim the fringe atmosphere off of stars." He said it as though it meant something. It didn't—at least not to me. But then, science had never been one of my strong points.

I floated there, not knowing what to say. He was gazing at me expectantly, so I finally told him the truth. "I don't understand. So you skim the fringe atmosphere off of a star and don't get melted to slag—so what? What good is it?"

Vimister chucked again. Reaching into a pouch in his shirt, he removed a small object, shielding it from my view with his hand. Then, suddenly, he whipped his hand back.

For an instant, I thought he held a miniature star.

The light dazzled me. Then it slowly faded and I could could see what he really held—a red-gold jewel the size of my thumb. But what a jewel! I'd never seen its like before—it was cut in a dozen facets, like any standard diamond, only in each facet hung a sapphire-like star . . . and each star was a different color! I gaped at it.

Finally, I managed to shut my mouth. "But— How—"

Vimister Groll tucked the jewel back into his pouch. "Trade secret," he said with a chuckle. "You can see why we need guards posted all over the *Falcon*. There are spies from other trader ships aboard. It's best to discourage them."

"Tell me who they are," I said quickly. "I'll have them stranded on Losal. If news of this gets out—"

"It already has," Ulega said. "There's nothing we can do, except take precautions and prevent the actual method of processing from leaking."

"Besides," Vimister said, "it's not cricket . . . er, polite . . . to throw other ships' spies off."

Another weird Free Trader custom. "You'd rather shoot them?" I asked sarcastically. "The armed guards are a bit obvious."

He shrugged. "A mere show of force, nothing more. Any spy stupid enough to get caught by one of the guards probably deserves what he gets. No, we let the spies remain on board because we know who they are and can watch them. If we threw them off, others would simply replace them . . . and we might miss one. That we can't risk."

"I don't understand," I said, "and I don't think I ever will. I'd think it best to make sure there are no spies on board at all."

"It's not your decision."

"As you say. You've hired me to do a job, and I'll do it better than anyone else you could've hired." That I felt sure of. I glanced once around the room where I was still floating. "Now, if you'd be kind enough to let me down, I have work to do."

Vimister Groll moved one of his hands a fraction of an inch, touching some hidden control. The room grew dark and spun crazily, then it settled down and I was standing on the deck again. Stepping forward, I found myself in the corridor—this time alone.

I leaned against the gray wall panels for a minute, eyes closed, while relief washed through me. Taking a deep breath, I forced myself to relax. The stasis field took a lot out of people, and I felt completely drained. Though I knew why the Ship's Council had used it, it still irritated me that they'd felt the need.

Still, I understood their caution with new members of the crew. They were skimming the fringe atmosphere off stars—nothing illegal, but certainly something that warranted extra precautions. My fears had proved to be unfounded, and for that I was grateful to Ghu and whatever other gods look after starship captains.

Now, I thought, to see about running my ship.

I levered myself up into the control seat. The nullspace power screen crackled with electricity as it descended over my head—an invisible curtain of energy. I plugged into the ship's computer. Instantly, it seemed, the air around me came to life. Jags of gold and silver danced across the distant horizon and blue sparks hung like scattered sand before me. The sparks were stars, I knew, and the sweeping currents on the horizon were the ether streams of nullspace. I felt a thrill of elation. Although I would not be the one guiding the ship into the currents of nonexistence, it was my duty to monitor our progress—and to cut in if anything went wrong. In the meantime, I could enjoy the spectacle before me.

"Kel," I heard a distant voice say. It took me a minute to realize where it had come from—and that Luathek had said it.

I slipped out of the interface. The computer-enhanced images faded from my eyes. When I blinked, I saw the huge, spherical control room once more. It was around twenty meters in diameter, filled with the monitoring equipment that made sure we'd make it through nullspace safely. Lights blinked reassuring greens and yellows. Machines made small, friendly beeping noises. Viewscreens showed black space dotted with stars.

There was no "up" or "down" here, no repellers gave

the illusion of gravity. The gray-uniformed techs all floated, weightless, at various angles—some head-up in relation to me, some head-down. They moved across the controls and monitors like insects over flowers. Since I'd been raised on-planet, as a cadet it had taken me a while to get used to the odd sense of direction in zero-gee space. But that had been fifteen years ago, and the *Falcon*'s control room offered no problems of perception for me now.

To my left floated Luathek.

He bobbed his four eyestalks once in greeting. His skin was a vibrant gray—flushed darker than usual with excitement. But he managed to restrain himself enough to ask, "Kel, are things fine with your working?"

"Yes," I said. "Everything's okay. But I can tell you're excited. What job did the computer assign you to?"

"First Tech, maintenance!" His eyestalks writhed with pride.

"Great!" I said. The job title meant Luathek would be in charge of all maintenance on the vessel, and I knew he'd keep the machinery running if it were at all sentiently possible. But, even better, as a First Tech he held a job roughly equivalent to that of an officer . . . and I'd be able to socialize with him legitimately. I knew some Ship's Councils frowned on close relations between captains and non-ranked crew.

"I can not stay long here, Kel," Luathek said. "I must return to my many duties and begin inspectations."

"Good idea," I said, smiling secretly at his bizarre word choice. "I've still got a lot to do here myself."

Turning, he grabbed a metal rung and pulled himself toward the door. I turned back to the nullspace power field interface.

Life quickly settled into routine. The crew got used to

me and I to them. I began to dig through the paperwork that had piled up while the *Marrow Falcon* hadn't had a captain to take care of such things. Luathek reported to me in confidence that the *Falcon* was in first-class condition, so I didn't have to worry about that.

In addition, the Ship's Council provided me with confidential documents giving the technical details of starskimming, though I didn't begin to understand most of it. Briefly, it goes something like this:

A pair of shuttles, carrying nullspace generator equipment, set out for a sun. The shuttles enter nullspace—where the stars are cooler—and pass close to the target sun, using gravity funnels to isolate a bit of the sun's hydrogen atmosphere. Then they carry the super-heated hydrogen back to the *Marrow Falcon* (keeping it in nullspace) and turn it over to the processing station, which combines it with various other elements in a fusion reactor. The end product is a super-hard, super-beautiful jewel that glows with an inner light . . . a jewel the like of which the universe has never seen before.

The Council had a whole schedule set up. In six months, the first jewels would go on sale to a few select customers. In eight months, the whole universe would be screaming for them. In ten months, they'd go on sale to the general public—to anyone who had enough royals to buy them. The Free Traders would make them pay a thousand times a king's ransom for every cut gem . . . and I knew they'd get it.

It was on the fourth day that preparations for slipping back into normal space began. In an unusually cheerful mood, I called a greeting to a couple of techs as I entered the control room's hatch and grabbed the nearest rung, pulling myself toward my command chair. The techs nodded back politely, and one even waved. They had truly accepted me, I realized.

For once, I didn't even mind the black-and-red-uniformed guard floating next to the hatch. Today the *Falcon* would enter the Xelthufed system and take up orbit around a red giant. Today would be the first real test of my skill as commander. I looked forward to it.

A low gong sounded.

Tech Shucel Baref—whom I'd found to be a competent worker and an excellent Moopsball player, as well as a witty conversationalist—turned and said, "Ten minutes to realspace slip, Captain Corrian."

"Thank you," I said. I activated the computer and its information grid hovered on the edge of perception. I focused on it for an instant, watching its timer count down the minutes, then the seconds.

Finally, the moment came. The counter reached zero. My hands poised over the controls, ready to take over from the computer if a system failure occurred and the automatic equipment didn't work. The computer's tactical grid flooded my senses with information.

I saw the *Falcon* from a dozen different angles at once, twisting its way through a long, dark tunnel. Scattered sparks of light and non-light whisked by and vanished in the distance. I felt myself falling a thousand different directions at once—and struggled to focus my thoughts and energies. I had to be aware of everything, conscious of every variation in the nullspace power fields in case anything went wrong.

The strain of keeping my thoughts in order was staggering. All my life I'd heard horror stories of captains who'd lost their minds while looking into the shifting patterns of nullspace.

"Slip . . . now, sir," Shucel said.

I felt the familiar disorientation begin around me. Colors shifted: red to orange, orange to yellow, green to blue—all up and down the spectrum. Sounds were muted and strange. Time seemed to stretch on and on. My muscles bunched painfully. I felt myself beginning to sweat. Then the colors flipped back to normal and we were through—with one of the smoothest slips into normal space I'd ever felt.

A cheer went up among the techs. I grinned and relaxed, leaning back. "A nice job," I said. "Good work."

They acknowledged my praise with smiles of their own as they turned back to their instruments. I could see the star Xelthufed on several of the viewscreens—an angry, brooding, blood-red sun, already swollen several times as large as Earth's Sol. It wouldn't have too many million more years left before it went nova or collapsed into itself—not that it mattered much to me.

"Solar flares?" I asked.

"Minimal, sir," Jamis Lore, a Second Tech, answered.

"Good. Take up position 200 million kilometers from the surface, stationary."

"Yes, Captain."

The ship's engines came to life—a dull vibration that passed through the hull around me. The *Falcon* surged ahead. Xelthufed grew larger on the viewscreens, the sensors automatically screening down its brilliance to a tolerable level.

"Any sign of other ships?" I asked, thinking of the spies the Ship's Council had said were on board. If one had managed to get a message off the ship before we entered nullspace. . . .

"Scanning . . . no, sir. Nothing out there but gas and rock."

"Good." I was suddenly very tired. "Keep a watch for other vessels."

The engines cut out and I knew we were coasting.

"Time to orbit— three hours, twelve minutes, sir," Jamis said.

"Captain Corrian. . . ." The intercom at my left ear whispered. It was a man's voice, soft and hesitant. I was puzzled. This was a closed channel, access permitted only to Ship's Council and top officers. Yet, I didn't remember this voice.

Touching "mute," I sub-vocalized to keep our conversation private until I could find out who this was. "Yes."

"My name is Jol Mellawithe, sir. I'm a scientist. I work for Vimister Groll. I must talk to you. The ship's in terrible danger!"

I stiffened, my previous feeling of exhaustion drowned in a rush of adrenaline. Was this some malcontent? One of the spies? "What are you doing on this channel?" I demanded. "It's restricted."

"Never mind that, sir! A little bit of rewiring the intercom in the rec hall did it. I must speak to you, Captain!"

"Why didn't you say something to me sooner? I've been here quite a while."

"They've been keeping me drugged, sir. I know it now! At first, I thought I was sick. My head hurt—I could scarcely think. As soon as I stopped eating the food they brought me, I-I recovered. You must believe me! The ship's in terrible danger!"

"What do you mean?"

"Not over this channel, please, sir. Can you meet me in the rec hall?"

I hesitated. He seemed to be raving. Did I want to be seen with him? "Why not someplace more private?"

"All the cabins are bugged. I don't want them to hear us, sir. I'm taking a terrible chance now! Please, Captain Corrian?"

With a shrug, I made my decision. "I'll be in the rec hall in five minutes." I snapped the intercom button off and stood. "Page me if any problems come up," I said to the techs on duty.

Then I headed for the door and the recreation hall three levels below.

I stood in the doorway to the rec hall, looking down the row of game areas and gym equipment. A couple of off-duty maintenance men played Moopsball on a holofield. A pair of techs played Rat and Dragon near the far wall. Over on the far side of the room, at a small table, sat a tall, thin man with wild-looking, uncombed, gray hair. He kept glancing around the room as though expecting troops to break through the bulkheads and arrest him at any moment. I knew at once that this had to be Jol Mellawithe even before he noticed me and motioned me over with a nervous wave of his hand.

Crossing the intricately patterned tile floor, I sat down opposite him. He touched the table's controls and raised a shimmerscreen around us, creating a private booth.

"You wanted to see me," I said, "and I'm here. What's all this about danger to the ship?"

"You *must* stop the starskimming, sir!" he cried, clutching at me. "There are aliens living in this star! They'll kill us all if you don't!"

"Wait a minute! Calm down," I said, coldly detaching his hands from my shirt. "Who's living in the star?"

"Aliens, sir! I-I detected them myself!"

"How?" I demanded.

"I've been working with the starskimming equipment. Once, when I set up the grav funnel, I accidentally tapped into their communications net. It's—"

The shimmerscreen around us suddenly crackled and

dissolved, sending blue and red sparks streaming in all directions. Ulega Max stood there, flanked by four tall guards. I'd been so engrossed in Jol Mellawithe's story that I hadn't noticed Ulega's approach.

"Take him," Ulega Max said to the guards. They moved forward and seized Jol by the arms, dragging him from his chair.

"Wait!" I roared. The guards stopped, a bit to my surprise. Angrily I turned to Ulega Max. "What's the meaning of this?"

"This man's sick," he said.

Jol clutched the gold medallion around his neck and shouted, "I am not—I swear by Ghu—aliens are there!"

Aliens in stars? It sounded crazy, and Jol certainly didn't look any too sane. But I was getting sick and tired of Ulega trying to run my ship!

"Be quiet," I told Jol sharply, "and I'll get to the bottom of this." He shut up. Then I faced Max. "Explain, Ulega. Now! What's this about?"

"It's true that Mellawithe works—worked—for us. He was on the team that first surveyed this system. He claimed he found traces of an alien communications net when he did a spectroscopic analysis of the star, but nobody could verify his report and the matter was dropped. I thought he'd dropped it, too, but it would appear not. Fortunately, I had him watched. He's unstable and needs to be sedated until proper treatment can be arranged."

"No!" Jol shouted. He began to struggle against the guards, who only tightened their grips. "I'm not crazy, sir! It's true! It's true!"

I motioned to the guards. "Take him to the ship's hospital and get him calmed down." I knew we'd never get anything accomplished with him shouting like that.

"Yes, Captain," one said. Then they half-led, half-dragged their writhing captive off and out the door. I watched in silence.

"A good move," Ulega said. "Quick, decisive. I like that. We can get on with our work now."

"Now we can talk," I said sternly. "You say his claims were never verified?"

"No. We devoted weeks to research, but couldn't find a trace of Mellawithe's so-called aliens. There's simply nothing and no one there. I trust you won't pay any attention to him. He's obviously deluded. Space crazed."

"I'll keep your opinions in mind," I said.

This was obviously not the answer he wanted. Ulega frowned. "I—"

"Please give me a moment to think," I interrupted. This was too important a decision to be rushed.

Ulega said his men had checked out Jol's report. But, I wondered, just how hard would they have looked if they knew discovering a sentient race would cut into profits. Surely, finding a new life form would weigh more—even with Free Traders—than a few million royals! At least, I hoped so.

There was another alternative to consider. What if Jol were a spy trying to delay our starskimming? I shook my head. What could he possibly gain from it . . . except time?

Time to bring in *his* people?

Ulega cleared his throat irritably. "The Ship's Council expects to start skimming as soon as possible," he snapped. "You're wasting time. You need to order the shuttles launched—we've almost reached our position."

He was efficient to the last. Not thirty seconds had passed since Jol Mellawithe had been here screaming at us about aliens. Already he'd moved on, begun planning something else, and he expected me to keep up.

I didn't think there were aliens living in the star. But if

there was even a chance. . . .

"Well, Captain?" Ulega said.

I decided Jol Mellawithe was either crazy or a spy. I'd traveled most of the galaxy and never heard of creatures living in a star. There was too much at stake to stop now. *Turn to page 58.*

It's not wise to take chances, I reminded myself. We'd move on to another star. That would set back the schedule and cut into profits, probably make the Ship's Council furious. But if there's even a chance that there are sentient creatures living in Xelthufed, it's worth it. *Turn to page 67.*

STARSHIP CAPTAIN CORRIAN

I shook my head sadly, knowing I could never accept the captainship of the *Marrow Falcon* under Ulega Max's terms. "No," I said. "I'm sorry, but I can't take the job—it would be too great a risk. Perhaps, if you'd tell me more about the ship, I'd change my mind."

His face grew red with anger. "It's classified Ship's Business! You'll know when you take the captainship, not a moment sooner. Trust me. This would be a good captainship for you . . . and we'd certainly make it worth your time. If nothing else, think of the money—a secure financial future. You'd like that, wouldn't you?"

"But I can't afford to trust you. You'll have to find someone else." I turned to go. "Come on, Luathek."

The Free Trader shouted, "Corrian, I'm warning you—"

I whirled. "If you threaten me, Ulega Max, I'll report you to the Patrol. There are witnesses present." I glanced pointedly at Luathek. "Just let us leave peacefully, and you'll be able to continue your search for a new captain without any complicated legal delays. Or costly lawsuits."

"Go then," he snapped. "May your trade goods rot and your ship fall apart beneath you!"

"Thanks," I said. "I wish you all luck, too."

Then Luathek and I stalked out into the corridor, back the way we'd come. Jespar Melsif followed us. His manner was quiet, subdued, almost apologetic. But I knew he'd come along to watch us, to act as a guard. A little sabotage in the right places could strand a shuttle on-planet for several weeks—a fate worse than death to Free Traders. Not to mention all the extra expense it would cause.

Still, we would never have done anything to the *Marrow*

Dart, as much as I might think about it, and I resented Jespar's presence. I held no bitterness toward the shuttle or her crew. Disappointment, yes—but no anger.

In the airlock, Jespar caught my arm. "Wait," he said softly.

"Yes?"

"I . . . wish to express my regrets. Ulega Max is under great strain. He meant no harm."

"We understand," I said.

"Ah . . . ?"

When I finally saw what he wanted, I had to laugh. "Don't worry, I have no intention of going to the Patrol with a complaint against him. As far as I'm concerned, the matter is over. Let's see that it stays that way."

"Thank you, Citizen," he said. With a short, awkward bow, he turned and went back into the ship.

Luathek and I continued down the entry ramp to the concrete landing field. Losal's sun was setting, and the rows of tall, sleek shuttles and starships seemed more impressive than ever, as they stood silhouetted against the orange and pink sky. A cool wind blew from the west, making me shiver, and I realized I'd been sweating while inside the ship. Suddenly, all the tension drained from my body, leaving me weak and exhausted.

A transit platform, having noticed us, pulled up. Luathek stepped on and grabbed the control railing. I followed him.

"Destination?" the platform asked.

"The main gate," I said.

"Please hold on tightly."

When we did so, the platform started forward, rising two feet above the ground with a whir of its repellers. It sped between the rows of tall, sleek shuttles and starships, banked smoothly to the right, and glided to a stop in front of the huge gates where we'd entered the landing field—what now seemed ages ago.

"Thank you for using me," said the platform as we stepped down.

"You are most welcome," Luathek replied.

With a whir, the transit platform rose and flew off to the left.

A Centaxi—the same one as before?—stood on guard duty at the gate, its hundreds of cilia writhing. Two of its noses clicked and blinked, and it shifted toward us. I'd never been able to figure out how their sensory organs worked. Only when it faced me did I notice the translator-box implanted in the middle of what might've been its chest. It would be able to talk with us.

Since I didn't see any way to get back to Boorgwal's Tavern other than walking, I approached the Centaxi. Its cilia writhed endlessly.

"Citizen," I said, "can you call a flitter for us?"

"Rrumph-ph-ph (*click*)," it said, shaking its cilia. "Dat ees down, See-tee-sen. Eet cowm soon."

"Uh, thank you," I said. Not knowing anything about Centaxi protocol (and certainly not about to shake appendages), I bowed.

The Centaxi's cilia only writhed. It said nothing more.

Within minutes a small flitter swooped down and landed five meters away. With a hiss, its door swung open. We climbed inside, then the door shut.

A strangely familiar voice said, "Please insert your identicard and state your destination."

I did so. For a second, nothing happened—and then the flitter's computer began to laugh. It was an awful sound, like the watery coughing of some huge sea creature. Unable to help myself, I shivered. Then I realized this flitter was the same one that had tried to cheat me earlier!

What terrible luck! Irritably, I pressed the handpad and tried to open the door. I found it locked. Sealed shut. We couldn't escape.

The flitter's engines roared to life, then it lifted into the air. Gravity gyrated wildly as we jerked forward, stopped, plunged three feet down, jerked forward again. Luathek moaned, his eyestalks turning a sickly gray. I didn't feel so well, either.

Seizing the seat in front of me, I pulled myself forward, toward the control box on the cabin wall. The flitter swooped to the left. I bounced off the seat to my right, then managed to scramble to the front of the passenger compartment. The floor seemed to drop out from under me. Swallowing quickly, I tried not to throw up. Then I managed to reach the control box. Swinging back the covering grid, I punched the large green button in its middle, activating the safety web—something that passengers were only supposed to do in case of an imminent crash.

Thick strands of some rubbery substance shot from hidden slots in the floor and ceiling, wrapping around my body, forcing me down and tying me to a seat. Behind me, I heard sounds of Luathek being similarly subdued. Now we couldn't possible be thrown forward or back, and only then did I sigh with relief.

"I am thanking you, Kel!" Luathek called up to me.

The flitter's evil laughter stopped. It must've realized it couldn't hurt us any more, for it settled down and flew a more normal course, weaving insect-like among the skyscrapers toward our destination. Soon we reached Boorgwal's Tavern, and there the flitter lowered itself to ground level. The hatch opened with a hiss, the safety web retracted, and we could move again.

Unsteadily, I got to my feet and climbed out. The flitter's computer spat my identicard at me. I caught it, then tucked it into my pouch.

"I— You—" I was literally speechless with rage.

"I've deducted my fee," it said. "Fifteen royals, as agreed, plus a five royal tip for excellent service." It didn't give me a chance to argue, but slammed its hatch closed and lifted before I could even begin to think of taking down its registration number. I blinked, and it was gone.

Luathek tugged on my arm. "Come on, Kel. I wish to imbibe a drink."

"Yes," I said heavily. "Me, too."

With a sigh, I pushed through the shimmerscreen door and entered the tavern after Luathek. The place hadn't changed during our absence—the lights were still dim, the temperature still warm, the crowd of pleasure-seekers still quiet and sedate. Even the shimmerscreened booths still held the same people, the flickering neon signs outside them advertised for the same jobs: two navigators, a lieutenant, some mercenaries . . . did it ever change? Several booths—including Luathek's and mine—stood empty.

In minutes, another neon sign would be added to the others—the new one saying "captain." Would it never be turned off? I wondered bitterly. If only I'd waited and jumped ship on a truly civilized world, a world near one of the main trade routes. . . .

Luathek winced at the pain in my thoughts. "Kel . . ."

"Sorry," I said, and I made an effort to shield my despair from him.

"Hey, you two," someone called. "Corrian, Luathek! Come here."

Slowly, we turned. The human bartender grinned and motioned for us to join him, so we headed in his direction. Luathek hopped up onto a stool in front of the realwood bar while I stood, leaning on the counter. The bartender— his nametag said "Rem Fantom"—nodded cordially, saying, "This is for you. It's already been paid for." Then he produced two large glasses filled with a warm, spiced, amber liquid called purten. The natives of Losal considered it a delicacy.

"What?" I said, surprised. "Paid for? By whom?"

He shrugged. "Didn't say. Free Traders. Maybe friends of yours?"

I shrugged. Free Traders? Then I realized that the drinks had to be from Ulega Max—a gesture of apology. Purten was too sweet for my tastes, but it was free, so I drank with an appreciative murmur. Luathek drained his glass at once, smacking his lips in delight. He liked the stuff.

New customers were few this time of day. Rem Fantom leaned forward to talk. I didn't mind. Fantom was an odd character. His long black hair had been oiled down and combed straight back over his head, and the tips of his moustache had been waxed and twirled into little spirals. That, combined with a red and black uniform that looked like something out of a historical vid, gave him an oddly timeless appearance, as though he'd always been in Boorgwal's Tavern and always would be. His age was unguessable. I couldn't help but wonder how long he'd worked here. He seemed as much a part of the atmosphere as the flickering neon lights or the shimmerscreen booths.

"Those Free Traders were just in here looking for you, Corrian," he said.

"Oh?" I stared at him in surprise. "How long ago?"

"Not long."

I paused. Perhaps Ulega Max and his assistant had reconsidered their offer, come to answer my questions about the *Falcon*. At least, I hoped so! Our prospects didn't look too bright right now.

"Can you describe them?"

He shrugged. "They all look the same to me. Once you've seen one Free Trader. . . ."

"I know what you mean." I tried to contain my impatience.

"They were looking for a new captain."

That *had* to be Ulega Max! Shrugging, I said, "Oh, I talked to them already. That's where I've been for the last couple of hours. They wouldn't tell me anything about their ship, so I turned down the job."

"No, I don't mean the ones you left with earlier. *Those* Traders I remember. You made a wise move, in my opinion. A more sinister-looking lot I've never seen. No, these three came in about an hour ago, saw you'd gone, and became quite frantic about it. They began questioning everyone in the place—annoying people, as you can imagine—and I finally had to tell them you'd left with another bunch of Free Traders. They got rather upset. Then I threw them out."

"No!" I said, aghast.

"Yes!" He laughed. "But, since you and Luathek have been such good customers, I got them to leave a message first and buy you drinks, in case you came back." Reaching under the counter, he felt around and finally drew out a battered old message tape. "Of course, all the time I spent getting the tape took away from my duties, and my tips suffered mightily as a result. . . ."

With an unvoiced sigh, I produced my identicard. I couldn't really afford it, but I could hardly refuse him money after all he'd done for us. "Why don't you give yourself a couple of royals for your trouble?" I said.

"Most kind, most kind, Citizen," he murmured. He slipped the card into a slot in the bar and made the transfer from my account. As he returned it, he said, "There's an old reader in the back room. You're welcome to use it, if you want."

"Thanks." I picked up the tape and turned to go.

"Wait," he said. "There's also this." He produced a spaceport pass like the one Ulega Max had given me. Taking it, I nodded appreciatively.

To show I was in no hurry, I made myself walk to the back room's door (Luathek almost tripping on my heels), pushed it open, entered, waited for it to close, then ran as fast as I could to the reader and shoved the tape into the scanning slot. It clicked into place, and I pushed the Read button.

Nothing happened. The screen remained completely blank, powerless.

"Kel," Luathek said, pointing, "there is a slot on this side. Perhaps one must, before reading, insert an identicard?"

"Huh?" I looked and, sure enough, someone had installed an identicard slot. It cost money to use the reader . . . but then, I'd never seen a bar that gave anything away for free, beyond a drink or two on rare occasions. Sighing, I slipped my identicard into the slot.

A grating voice said, "To use this reader, a charge of three royals must be paid in advance. Shall I deduct it from your card?"

"Yes," I snarled.

The reader clicked to itself for several moments. "It has been done. I will now play the tape."

Eagerly, I watched the screen. Beside me, Luathek, too, gazed at it, his eyestalks twitching with excitement.

Finally, an image appeared—that of a small, thin human male with long blond hair and dark green eyes. I assumed he was a ship's owner, since he wore a plain black dress uniform, without insignia of any kind. And yet there was something odd about him . . . for a trader, he didn't look right—he didn't have the in-bred look of sameness of the Free Traders. Perhaps he was an independent?

He started to speak, but then the picture disintegrated into wavy lines and colorful bursts of static. A garbled, choking sound came from the speaker.

I stared at Luathek. Luathek stared back at me.

"It must be having a bad track scanner," he said. "I will fix it."

Taking a small screwdriver from his pouch, he opened the back of the reader and began tinkering with its insides. The picture faded. The sound stopped. Abruptly, a grating voice said,

"To use this reader, a charge of three royals is . . . is . . . is. . . ."

"Ah!" the Pavian said. "The problem is most visible to me. Now . . . it is fixed!"

Suddenly the message tape whirred in the scanner— rewinding, I guessed. Luathek set the back of the reader into place again. The tape started for the second time, only now the reader had no trouble. The picture came up at once, and the black-uniformed man spoke.

"Greetings, Citizens Corrian and Foraligon. My name is Jawn Kessel, and I own the trade ship *Trim Dreamer*. In the chance you might still be unemployed, and that you might return to Boorgwal's Tavern, I have left this tape in the hands of the bartender, along with a spaceport pass made out in your names. I wish to offer you both positions in my crew.

"If you are interested, please come to the spaceport at once. My shuttle is the *Trim Screamer*. Thank you."

And then the image winked out. I fingered the spaceport pass and grinned. We'd found another job after all!

"Kel?" Luathek said. "I hope you do not mind, but I wish to—er—*walk* to the spaceport this time."

"Good idea," I said. "Let's go!"

The trip took almost an hour by foot—but fortunately this was one of the safest cities in the League, and we had no problems with the natives. At last we stood before the eastern gates. A gray-furred Jurisnac, looking like a cross between a dog and a bear, took the pass and motioned us through. A transit platform delivered us quickly to the *Trim Screamer.*

The arrowhead-shaped shuttle was clean, but old and run-down, looking like it had served its owner well for many years. The ramp lay extended, so we walked up to the airlock, pushed the call button, and settled back.

We didn't wait long. Soon the external airlock doors opened and Kessel appeared. He was almost my height—taller than he'd appeared on the message tape—and he grinned at me warmly.

"Kel Corrian and Luathek elt Foraligon—I'm so glad you came!" He took my hand and shook it in that quaint old-fashioned style some traders liked to affect. "Please, come aboard!"

"Thank you, Citizen Kessel," I said, and Luathek echoed my words.

We followed him through the airlock and into a small corridor that had an open hatch at the far end. Through the hatch, I could see another corridor, this one with numerous doors opening off it. Kessel went through first, turned to the door immediately on the right, and touched the handpad. The door dilated, and he stepped through, motioning for us to follow.

It was his personal cabin, I saw at once. Rich gold and red tapestries decorated the walls, and the furniture was the elegant sort only a ship's owner would be able to afford. Soft music came from hidden speakers, and I smelled the unmistakable scent of pines. As we sat around a small glass table, in comfortable all-form chairs, Kessel dialed up cool fruit drinks from the auto-bartender. Only after he'd sipped his bayafruit punch did he speak.

"I suppose you know I want to hire you?"

I nodded. Luathek said, "Yes."

"Well, I don't know what offer Ulega Max made— Oh, yes," he said in answer to my look of astonishment, "I did some checking on where you went when I didn't find you in the employment bar. At any rate, I know I can't match Max's offer financially. However, there are a lot of benefits to working on a small trade ship like the *Trim Dreamer.* The crew is friendly, the atmosphere is more relaxed, the pace is slower, there's not as much stress. And I can use you both to your full ability."

"What happened to your last captain?" I asked.

Kessel made a disgusted noise. "He fell in love with a tavern girl, resigned his captainship, bought the tavern where the girl worked, and set himself up for life. He wants to be a proper groundirt Citizen now, won't have anything to do with starships—except to take money from their crews, of course. I've got a regular fifteen-planet trade route, and I need to find a new captain tonight if we're even going to have a prayer of making the next planet on schedule."

"I'll need more information on your ship."

"She's a Class IV Scout—a refurbished Patrol ship," he said with stiff-backed pride. "The crew'll number thirty-four, with you and Luathek. Our cargo is mainly food-stuffs, and we specialize in perishable goods . . . fruits, some grains, and so on. We've never had any trouble with the Patrol, we don't smuggle anything. The life's routine, but satisfying. I enjoy it."

"And Luathek?"

"The engineers who keep the *Dreamer* running have been asking for a stardrive technician for several months. They've been having trouble with the ship's nullspace generators and say we need a specialist. Oh, yes, we can certainly use you, Luathek!"

I looked at the Pavian. He nodded quickly.

"All right," I said. "We'll take the jobs. Base salary with the standard bonus and raise clauses?"

He grinned and nodded. "Great! So it's all settled. I've taken the liberty of scheduling our take-off for"—he glanced at his watch. —"ten minutes from now. Everything's been taken care of—course laid into the computer, clearance obtained, everything. Your duties will start in the morning."

"What about our gear?"

"It's already aboard."

I raised an eyebrow. "What if we'd turned down your offer?"

"Then I wouldn't be going anywhere, would I? Now, speed is of the essense. We must lift at once!" He stood. "You must be tired. I'll show you to your cabins."

"Thanks," I said, suppressing a yawn. "I could use a rest."

It had been a long day, but I was happy with everything we'd accomplished. The *Trim Dreamer* sounded like a good ship, and I knew I wouldn't regret my decision to captain her.

The *Trim Dreamer* was a good ship—smooth-running, easy to control—a pleasure on all counts. Luathek soon had her nullspace generators running as good as new, and over the first week we made a half-dozen nullspace slips with only the barest trace of field distortion. And he promised me (miracle worker that he was) that those distortions would soon be gone. The only draw back was her limited range—she could only slip fifteen light-years at a time before returning to realspace. But a series of slips could be made quickly, and we got to our destinations soon enough for Jawn Kessel. I rather enjoyed the relaxed pace.

In the third week of my captainship, when I'd adjusted myself to the ship's routine, I came to the control room to monitor the next realspace slip. The circular room hummed with life, as if always did when we were about to maneuver. Techs sat at their stations, monitoring all the equipment, and I oversaw their actions. Things went well.

The computer beeped softly in my left ear, signalling the approaching end of a nullspace slip. "Ten seconds, sir," one of the techs said.

When the moment arrived, we slipped into realspace. Colors blurred, shifted—red to orange, orange to yellow, green to blue—all up and down the spectrum. Then suddenly everything clicked back to normal. In an eyeblink, the universe was sane again.

I slipped into the computer's navigational screen, following the course of our ship against the background of stars. Off to our right floated a red giant the charts identified only as Beta Dainis. It was a run-down star in its last phase of degeneration, and it had no planets. I found the *Trim Dreamer*'s position, compensated for drift, and slotted our course through the next nullspace window. The numbers flickered in the bottom left corner of the screen.

"Ready for nullspace slip," I said.

"Aye, sir," the techs called back from their various positions around the room.

"Wait, Captain!" a woman's voice shouted.

I put a hold on the computer, then slipped from its screen, letting the navigation screen's image fall away. "What?" I demanded.

Rooli Tebwah, my Gultinian Tech in charge of ship's communications, turned her dark head to face me. "Captain Corrian—I'm picking up a distress call."

"Odd . . ." I murmured. Who would be in such an off-track system like Beta Dainis? "Are you sure it's a current transmission?"

"Sir—it's coming from a ship thirty thousand klicks astern. She's broadcasting registration marks . . . her name's the *Marrow Falcon*."

"The *Falcon*?" I repeated, shocked.

"Yes, sir."

"Ah . . . put it on my screen."

The small viewscreen on the arm of my chair came to life. I found myself looking at Ulega Max's sweat-stained face. He jumped when he saw me, his shock apparent.

"You!" he croaked.

"I'm answering your distress call," I said. "Let me speak to your ship's captain—now!"

"She's dead."

"Then . . . you must tell me what's wrong."

Slowly, he shook his head. "That's classified Ship's Business. I'm not going to talk about it over the radio. Supply us with help and you will be suitably compensated."

I frowned. "If you want help, you're going to have to do better than that. For all I know, you might be pirates, waiting to loot my ship."

"Don't be ridiculous, Corrian. By all that's decent, you're obliged to come to our aid!"

"Not if you won't tell me why."

He bit his lip. There was an air of desperation about him, a helplessness that disturbed me. I realized that, whatever had happened, he'd lost control of the situation. And he had too much pride to admit it. Now he was torn by the decision he faced—should he tell me the truth and risk his ship's integrity, or should he refuse and risk losing my help? I could tell the choice pained him.

At last he reached a decision. "I demand your immediate assistance!" he said surily.

Loyalty to his ship had won. I didn't know what to say to him.

"Well, Corrian?" he asked. "Are you going to help us or not?"

I decided to help him. Despite Ulega Max's attitude, I had to think about his crewmen—surely I couldn't hold them responsible for his actions! If something was wrong, it was my duty to aid them. *Turn to page 169.*

I had to ignore his distress call. I had my own ship to consider. By all the laws in space, if he refused to tell me over the radio what his emergency was, I was in my rights to refuse to come to his aid. I would relay his distress call to the proper authorities. *Turn to page 180.*

ATTACKED!

I decided the ship had too much invested in the Xelthufed system to leave without proof of alien creatures inhabiting the star. Mellawithe's "evidence" was nonexistent. If other techs couldn't reproduce his results, then he'd been mistaken . . . deliberately or not, I couldn't say.

"I agree with you," I said to Ulega. "There's not enough cause to slow down the starskimming schedule. The shuttles will continue as planned."

He smiled slightly. "Good." Then he turned and left, his black cape fluttering around him.

Watching him, I found myself wondering what he would have done if he been captain himself. He was brusque to the point of rudeness, but seemed to hold his loyalty to the ship above all else—even his own pride.

And that made him dangerous. He'd never work for me or with me on anything unless it was to the ship's benefit. Fortunately, by law, I had just as much authority over the crew as the Ship's Council did. By himself, Ulega could be a problem, but never a threat. I could count on Vimister Groll and Yamal Hydrif to keep him in his place.

Smiling, I returned to the control room.

WELCOME, CAPTAIN CORRIAN.
STATUS AS FOLLOWS:

1) APPROACHING ORBIT POINT AROUND STAR XELTHUFED.

2) BLACKMARK SHUTTLES #2, #4 PREPARING FOR DEPARTURE.
NEW ORDERS?

"Yes," I answered. "Do a spectroscopic analysis of Xelthufed's energy output. I want a complete breakdown of light, energy—everything. No one is to see this report, or know it's being done, except me. All findings are classified confidential. Execute."

"As you command, Captain Corrian," the computer said.

I let the screen fade from view. If Jol Mellawithe had discovered aliens, I wanted to find out myself, just in case. It didn't pay to take unnecessary chances.

I felt the engines come to life once more.

Tech Shucel pulled herself over and floated before me for a second, waiting for my attention. "Captain," she said.

"Yes?"

"Stationary park in eight minutes, sir."

"Thank you."

As she returned to her post, I tapped the intercom button. "Shuttle Two," I called.

After a pause, a woman's voice near my left ear said, "Shuttle Two, Commander Lilen Omm speaking."

"This is Captain Corrian," I said. "Status?"

"Both shuttles ready to launch, Captain."

"Excellent," I replied. "Prepare to launch on my command." Glancing at the computer's clock, I added, "Five minutes to launch time."

"Verified, Captain," Omm responded. The intercom clicked. I knew she'd be strapping herself into her control seat, helping to make all the last-minute checks before take-off.

I told the computer to bring the holograph back up. Flickering silver lines filled the air in front of me for a second, then the picture materialized: a scaled-down version of Xelthufed and, far from it, a small silver cylinder that represented the *Marrow Falcon.* Two blinking red lights at either end of the ship marked the shuttles in their docking cradles.

The Falcon's engines increased their thrust away from the star. I could feel the heavier vibrations through the deck, almost feel them in the air as a small sensation of gravity began to drift people toward the far wall. It would soon pass.

Then the engines cut off. The computer reported we were in a stationary position two hundred million kilometers from the star. I pushed the intercom button.

"Launch shuttles."

"Shuttles launched, sir," came two replies. On the holograph two of the red dots left the *Falcon*—one from either end—and were moving slowly toward Xelthufed.

"Good. Keep us posted," I said. Leaning back in the chair, I ordered the small viewscreen in the arm of my chair to pick up the monitors on the shuttles. The first picture showed the *Falcon's* docking cradle receding in the distance: the round end of the ship came into view, then the whole of its cylindrical body. It was a magnificent view, one that never ceased to amaze me with its simple beauty.

I switched monitors and brought the interior of Shuttle Two on-screen. A tall, gaunt woman dressed in a plain black uniform sat in the command chair. A gold medallion of a double-helix hung around her neck. I guessed her to be Commander Omm. She noticed me and gave a brief nod, then turned her attention to the controls once more.

Blackmark Model shuttles are faster than just about any small ship. The two I'd send out—the *Marrow Dart* and the *Marrow Knife*—would get within starskimming range in a matter of only a few minutes.

"Nullspace slip . . . now," I heard Omm say. Then the viewscreen crackled with a thousand colors of static and I lost contact with the shuttle. Normal communications between ships didn't work in nullspace. I'd pick the shuttle up again when it slipped back into realspace near the star.

I waited.

Finally, both shuttles reappeared for an instant. On the holo they were two red dots that seemed to crawl across the star's surface, but I knew in reality that they were several hundred thousand meters away from its atmosphere. Their force shields would be ablaze with light, I knew, as they absorbed and deflected all the energy Xelthufed would be throwing at them. They would take a quick position reading, then slip back into nullspace to do the actual work.

"A magnificent sight, Kel," Luathek said. He was suddenly at my side. I hadn't heard him come in.

I smiled. "Almost worth the trip in itself. How are things going in your department?"

"More well than I had been expecting." His two front eyestalks twitched a bit in the Pavian equivalent of a shrug. "I would not have it otherwise."

Together we watched as the shuttles vanished from the holograph.

"Well, Luathek," I said, starting to rise, "we can get in a little Moopsball—"

"Captain," Jamis reported suddenly, "there's some unusual solar activity going on."

"Bring it up on the main viewscreen." I sat back down.

"Yes, sir." His hands danced over the controls and an instant later the large screen directly in front of my chair changed shots. Now it showed a screened-down close-up shot of a small corner section of Xelthufed . . . the area where the shuttles had been. As Jamis had said, there was a bit of solar activity—long streamers of hydrogen reaching far into the void.

I wondered, suddenly, if there was a relationship

between the shuttles starting to skim the star and its sudden flare . . . and I wondered if it would pose a threat to either Commander Omm or my ship.

As I watched, the first streamer broke like a whip snapped in two. The stray energy hurtled off into space—by a strange coincidence heading toward the *Falcon*. I had an uneasy feeling about it.

The uneasiness grew as the second, third, and fourth streamers broke away from the star and came straight at us! They contracted in size, becoming almost egg-shaped. Probes? Missiles? Emissaries from whatever race of creatures Jol Mellawithe had detected and tried to warn me about? I didn't know. I needed more information before I could do much. I certainly didn't want to start a war!

"Raise the force shield," I said suddenly.

"Captain?" Jamis said, startled. "The force shields, sir?"

"Damn it! Do it—now!"

"Yes, sir!" He flushed, knowing he was in for a well-deserved reprimand.

The viewscreens flickered with static as the monitors picked up the energy of the force shield surrounding the ship. I watched the ameoba-like whatever-they-weres approach in silence. They didn't seem to be slowing.

"Kel," Luathek whispered. "The flarings—they are alive!"

"What?" I demanded. "Are you sure?"

"Yes. I feel their emotions . . . I think. Their minds are not like yours or mine. They are most . . . strange to me."

They came closer . . . closer, moving at nearly half the speed of light. In seconds, they filled the whole viewscreen.

"Sound Yellow Alert," I said, leaning forward.

And then they reached the ship.

For a second, nothing happened. I began to relax.

Then, far off, in some distant part of the ship, I heard alarm claxons begin to wail. A dull boom followed—an explosion!

Then like tidewaters rushing in, blue sheets of electricity washed through the door, crackled across the control panels and around the room in a mad dance. Sparks leaped across the room like fireworks gone wild. Small fires blazed behind instrument panels, but automatic equipment smothered them in foam before they did much damage. Meters and dials swung wildly. People were screaming and floating about in panic.

"Keep calm!" I shouted, struggling to do so myself. "Stay at your posts!" I stood and kicked myself out to the middle of the room, where I slowly spun and surveyed the situation around me.

Sheets of blue electricity covered everything. Nobody could touch any of the controls. Several techs tried, then jerked back with sharp cries—nursing burned, blistered fingers. One by one the computer screens were going black. Lights flickered and went out. Equipment growled to a halt.

I began to grow afraid. My ship was coming apart around me! Who was attacking us in this strange way? What could they hope to gain from it?

Then, as suddenly as it had come, the electricity crackled and vanished.

Red and yellow emergency lights slowly blinked all around me. Men and women cradled burned hands to their chests. Several cursed softly.

Drawing a deep breath, I gathered my strength. No great damage had been done—the computers had shut down automatically when overloaded. They could be repaired and put online in minutes. Rather, I worried about the star-creatures . . . and what they were doing now, while we were temporarily incapacitated.

"Sound Red Alert," I said, drifting over to the one bank of status displays still working. Shucel Baref floated there, frantically typing commands into the computer—even the voice reader had broken. I hovered beside her as the alarm claxons rang out, shrill and bleak in the sudden near-silence.

Not far off, someone moaned. It was a desperate, hopeless sound.

"Bring up the status display," I said, trying to keep up a front of confident authority. I had to force myself to stand still, keep my head up, and my voice steady. I told Shucel my access number and she put it in, giving me full command of the ship.

As she typed, I turned to Luathek. "I want a damage report in ten minutes. Hurry!"

"Yes, Kel." He grabbed the nearest rung and quickly pulled himself toward the door.

I turned back to Tech Shucel. Suddenly, the computer before us whirred and brought up a new screen.

STATUS: SHIP UNDER ELECTROMAGNETIC ATTACK.

NULLSPACE GENERATORS NO LONGER OPERATIONAL
MAIN THRUSTERS OPERATIONAL.

RECOMMEND:

1) RETREAT
2) COUNTER ATTACK

SHIP'S ARMAMENTS STANDING BY.

NEW ORDERS?

"Retreat," I said immediately. "Full thrust away from the star."

Shucel typed. I felt rather than heard the engines roar to life, and I found myself drifting out toward the middle of the room as my inertia gave me a strange sense of false gravity. Snagging a wall run, I held it as I stared up at the viewscreen overhead.

The energy creatures had moved off a bit. Now they hovered a scant two thousand kilometers away, directly between the *Falcon* and Xelthufed, blocking our way. I didn't like them that close to us—they could strike at any moment and we'd be helpless to stop them.

They'd caught me unprepared the first time. I swore they'd never do it again. Still, the damage they'd done could have been worse—much worse. It looked as though they'd come just to have a look around, then left when their mission had been accomplished. Would they be planning their attack now?

The techs were taking apart the panels, checking the wires, plugging new modules into place, throwing breaker switches that had tripped when the electrical surges hit— all in a quick, well-trained manner. Suddenly, computers hummed to life around us.

"What are we going to do, sir?" Shucel asked, her voice tight with anger and fear.

"Wait for the shuttles to get back," I snapped too quickly and forced myself to speak calmly.

"I won't abandon them as long as there's a chance they're still alive."

And . . . after that?

I would attack the star-creatures, maybe scare them off. They had invaded my ship and damaged it. I was determined to get even. And then, after they'd been properly put in their place, we'd be able to safely resume the starskimming we had come for. *Turn to page 91.*

I'd try to negotiate with the star-creatures. Luathek said they were intelligent. Perhaps, if we could find a way to talk to them, we'd be able to work out a safe way to skim the star, or even open trade relations with them. *Turn to page 104.*

SHATTERED CRYSTALS, SHATTERED DREAMS

I decided it wasn't wise to take chances—after all, if an intelligent race lived in the star, I didn't want to endanger them by skimming the fringe atmosphere off their home. I had an image of some alien race coming to Old Earth to siphon off part of the ocean, somehow completely missing all signs of human civilization, and scooping up several dozen water-craft with attendant human beings by mistake. . . .

What would we humans have done if something like that happened? I could guess readily enough—declared war and attacked! I couldn't risk something like that happening here. We'd have to move on to another star.

"Well?" Ulega Max prompted.

"We're going to have to move to another star," I said.

"But the Council—"

"They hired me to safeguard the ship, and I'm going to do that no matter what. Even if that means going against your wishes."

He frowned. "You can be dismissed, Corrian."

"I know that, but I don't think I will be."

"Oh? And why not?"

I smiled. "You don't want to be caught in a battle any more than I do. You're a sensible man. Think of the money it would cost to fight these star-creatures, if they exist. And besides that, it'll only take a couple of days to choose another star and travel there. Such a time-loss is minor compared to how long it would take to hire a new captain. You spent three weeks finding me, didn't you? That's an awful lot of lost profits. You have to admit it makes sense to go along with me this time."

"You're too smart for your own good." Turning, he

stalked away.

I shrugged. I didn't like opposing him, but there was no way he could argue with my logic. Besides, I felt certain I'd made the right decision.

Slowly, I headed for the laboratory. I had a lot of things to do.

"Yes, Captain," First Tech Hoffing Doran said, "that makes perfect sense."

We'd discussed the problem of finding another star. I'd told him we needed one similar to Xelthufed, astronomically near-by, and without planets. And I'd told him why.

"How long will it take?"

"I can tell you now, sir, if you want."

"Oh?"

He smiled thinly. "I'm the one who selected Xelthufed as our first target, remember, sir? It was close—there were two runner-ups. One is a yellow dwarf named Aldema Proxima. It's not far from here, either, if I remember correctly. The other's Beta Dainis, a red giant in its third phase of degeneration . . . should go nova in a few hundred thousand years."

"Which one would be best for us?"

"Either, sir. Both. They're about the same, in terms of the necessary atmospheric conditions, and they're both off the regular trade-routes."

I hesitated, then picked one at random. "Aldema Proxima it is, then. Feed the coordinates into the navcomputer. I'll be in the control room getting ready. We'll slip as soon as possible."

"Got to keep the Ship's Council happy, eh, sir?"

"Ah, you know about them."

"Yes, sir." His voice dropped to a conspiratorial whisper. "You'd best watch yourself around that lot, Captain.

68

They're a tough bunch. Rumor has it they . . . eliminated the last captain."

Eliminated? I wondered. Surely it couldn't be true—the Ship's Council would've been careful enough not to let news of a murder (if there really had been one) leak out. This was the sort of ship's gossip it was best to ignore. The crew always liked to make up stories to worry themselves and their officers.

"Thanks for the warning," I said. "I'll be careful."

Returning to the controls, I floated over to the command chair, studying the techs around me as I did so. Shucel Baref was still busy at the communications station. I knew a half-dozen of the others on duty by name, and all the rest by face. Making a mental note to use the ship's hypno-teacher to learn the rest of them as soon as I could, I added it to the long list of mental notes I already had. Sighing, I shook my head. Starship captains had to be on call twenty-four hours a day.

Jamis had been waiting for me. Pushing off the far wall, he drifted over to my seat, then grabbed the rung to my left. He handed me a data chip.

"Captain, these are the coordinates you wanted. First Tech Doran had them shot up here."

I plugged the chip into the reader. Immediately, the star chart rose as a hologram before me. It showed a yellow dwarf, with two large rings of asteroid belts. No planets, no bodies larger than a twenty-kilometer-wide asteroid, sixty-two light-years from the nearest trade planet . . . perfect. The star's name was Aldema Proxima and it was a scant twelve light-years away. Even Ulega Max wouldn't be able to criticize the choice.

"It looks great," I said.

"Yes, sir. I've already plotted our course. There's a window coming up in eight minutes. I thought you'd want to take it."

I grinned at him. "You anticipate my every thought. Keep up the good work."

"Thank you, sir." With a quick salute, he returned to his post.

After popping out the data chip, I activated the computer's information grid and leaned back, letting the screen rise before me. The timer ticked off minutes. Eight, then five, then finally one. . . .

My hands poised over the controls. I watched the seconds glide away. The rush of adrenaline raised my pulse, quickened my breathing.

"Slip . . . now," I heard Jamis say in the distance.

From the ease of our first slip, I didn't expect any trouble, but I was prepared to take manual control if necessary. For an instant, I felt a growing sense of disorientation, then the colors around me shifted, bleeding into one another, each moving one shade down the chromatic scale, red to orange, orange to yellow, yellow to green. Then everything righted itself and I knew we'd made the transition safely. The *Falcon* cut through nullspace now. Technically, it no longer existed. We had completely left the "real" universe.

I withdrew into the computer's information grid a second time, checking over the ship's functions. The nullspace power field held up nicely; the drives' power feed read a bit high, but nothing unusual. I'd have the techs check it over when we realspaced.

Everything seemed to be going well.

I slipped out of the grid and nodded to the techs around the control room. "A smooth slip, as good as I've ever seen. Nice job."

The rest of the three-day trip passed uneventfully for the

most part. The crew remained in high spirits, the Ship's Council only sent me one brief memo—"It has been decided that we will withdraw from the Xelthufed system and skim a different star"—and I finally finished up all the paperwork that had accumulated while the *Falcon* didn't have a captain. Only one incident marred the otherwise-ideal passage, and that had to do with Jol Mellawithe.

I went to see him as soon as we entered nullspace. He was in the ship's hospital, under heavy sedation for nervous exhaustion, and as I stood beside his cocoon-like healing tube he didn't seem to recognize me.

"Jol," I said. "How're you feeling?"

He looked up at me for a long moment, then a strange light came into his eyes. He seemed to recognize my face for the first time. "Aliens . . . must warn . . . stars are their worlds. . . ." And then his eyes became vacant again. He drooled.

Stars are their worlds. . . . What an odd thing to say. I wondered what he meant. Obviously he wouldn't be able to tell me anything. I felt a touch of disappointment, then put it from my mind. I hadn't really come for information anyway, just to check up on him, make sure he was receiving the best possible care.

I looked at the monitor . . . and noticed that Ulega Max had ordered him kept under sedation until we reached our next port. That could be as long as a month, I realized, frowning. That seemed far too long a time, but the auto-doctor had approved the sedation.

I wondered, briefly, if Ulega was keeping Mellawithe drugged simply because I'd listened to him. Had Max decided it would be best to keep me away from Jol and his crazy theories to make sure things went smoothly? If I hadn't listened to Jol, would he be up and about now, rather than trapped in a healing tube?

It was a disturbing thought. Since I had no way of confirming or denying it—other than asking Ulega Max, which I had no intention of doing—I put it from my mind.

Sighing, I rose and looked around me. The "hospital" was a round room with a gleamingly sterile white floor and walls. Examination and treatment tables, with attendant tools and equipment, made the far side of the room a jungle of metal tubes, trays, wires, and flashing lights. Healing tubes (all curtained off from one another) completely filled the other.

Mellawithe was the only serious patient at the moment, and he lay in the tube nearest the door. Several auto-nurses hovered near him at all times, their box-like bodies gliding effortlessly across the floor. As the center of their attention, I knew Jol would be well cared for. Now he'd need time and rest more than anything else. I decided I'd made the right decision about having him confined.

"He must be allowed to sleep now, Captain Corrian," an auto-doctor said, startling me. It had sidled up when I wasn't looking.

The auto-doctor was a thin cylinder that walked on three triple-jointed legs. It had a ring of metal eyes, five hands for various medical instruments, and a strict, no-nonsense voice.

"Please keep me informed as to his condition," I said.

"As you instruct, Captain Corrian."

Slowly, I returned to the control room.

We took up orbit a scant eighty million kilometers from the blazing, gaseous surface of the star Aldema Proxima. The crew had all been drilled as to their duties in starskimming, and little remained for me to do except set the machinery in motion.

"Launch the shuttles," I told Shucel Baref.

She passed on the instructions. On the hologram in front of me, I watched the *Marrow Falcon* slowly rotating, a perfect cylinder. Then the huge steel doors on the docking bays swung open and two of the Blackmark-model shuttles slowly backed out. Their thrusters flamed for a minute as they maneuvered to a safe distance from their mothership.

Activating the small viewscreen in the arm of my chair, I picked up the monitor in the control room of the second shuttle. A tall, gaunt woman wearing a neat black uniform sat in the command chair. She was Commander Omm, a thirty-year veteran spacer. Noticing my presence on her screen, she gave a brief nod, then her attention returned to the controls before her.

Her lips were moving, but I heard no sound. I turned up the volume.

". . . for nullspace slip . . . now."

Then my viewscreen flickered with a brightly colored static, and I lost contact with Omm. Normal communications weren't possible in nullspace. I'd have to wait for the shuttles' return to realspace to pick her up again.

I returned my attention to the hologram before me. "Bring up the star," I said to the computer.

It obliged and I looked at a screened-down view of Aldema's flaming surface. The star seemed unusually quiet, there were no great flares, no sunspots. Two small, dark shapes appeared for an instant—on the holo they seemed to crawl across the star's surface like tiny insects. Then they winked out of existence again, and I knew they'd taken their cargo aboard and were on the way back to the *Falcon*. The whole process of scooping up Aldema's atmosphere hadn't taken more than five minutes.

As soon as the shuttles returned, the techs would start transforming the super-heated gas into those dazzling jewels. Then, if the initial processing went well, we'd begin full-scale skimming in the morning.

I found my excitement growing. Though I knew the technical details, I suddenly decided I wanted to see the actual manufacturing myself—at least for the first batch of jewels.

Taking the lift down to the proper level, I stepped out into a small, bare room with a guard on duty at the far end. He saluted me as I walked past, and I returned the gesture.

Upon entering the next room, I just stopped and stared. The pictures I'd seen on my control seat's monitor hadn't done the place justice. The huge, circular laboratory sprawled out before me. Thousands of machines filled the place. The hum of their engines sounded like millions of insects. All the equipment gleamed with chrome and polish. Small lights blinked and flashed all around me, signifying things I could only begin to imagine.

Dozens of white-uniformed men and women moved among the equipment, running tests, setting switches, doing whatever needed to be done in preparation for the shuttles' arrival.

A small brown-haired woman in a white lab coat stepped up to me. "Captain Corrian," she said, "I'm Tech Friesner. May I help you, sir?"

"No, no," I said quickly. "I'm just looking. I wanted to watch the jewels being made."

She turned to her left, nodding toward a large gray box-like machine. Huge steel tubes ran into its top from the ceiling and a conveyor belt extended from its near side. "That's the Radix Equalizer, sir," she said, "where the final refinements will take place. The shuttles have already docked and are unloading their cargo. The processing should start in just a moment."

A low gong sounded. I looked around, bewildered. but

Tech Friesner only smiled.

"That's the signal, sir," she said. "This way."

I followed her over to the Equalizer and joined the small crowd already gathered. The machine hummed faintly, and I could see it vibrating. Water began to condense on its sides and roll down to the floor where it formed a large pool. Small gratings in the floor suddenly popped open and sucked the water away.

I found myself straining to hear, straining to see. My breathing quickened. My pulse raced with excitement.

"This is it, sir!" Friesner whispered. Her voice rose with a strange intensity.

At last the conveyor belt began to move. Out of the machine rolled six perfectly cut jewels, each the size of a terrestrial hen's egg. The gems glowed white-hot.

Slowly the heat dissipated, leaving a row of six of the most beautiful jewels I'd ever seen. In each intricately cut facet hung a star of a different color. I stepped forward without thinking, drawn like a moth to a flame. The other techs pressed in close as well, eager to examine them.

"Back to your posts!" Friesner called. "There's lots more to be done today. You'll all have a time to see them later, when we're finished."

Grumbling, the men and women turned and hurried back to their posts. Tech Friesner watched them go. Only then did I notice what she now held: a small metal box with a stronglock on its side. I nodded in satisfaction, knowing we'd want to keep these little beauties safely locked away.

Without a second's hesitation, Friesner flipped back the box's lid, picked up the first gem, then nestled it among the foam padding. She stored the next four without a second's hesitation, but when she picked up the last one, she just held it for a long minute, staring deep into its heart.

"Is something wrong?" I asked at last.

She said nothing. Her face muscles grew slack, relaxed—like those of a child or someone asleep. I frowned, a bit disturbed. She seemed to have accidentally put herself in some sort of hypnotic trance.

Reaching out, I plucked the gem from her hand and set in into the box with the others. Then I flipped down the lid and dialed the stronglock closed.

"Tech Friesner," I said loudly.

Tech Friesner shook her head and her eyes found a focus. She grew aware of me. "What happened, sir?" she asked, confusedly.

"Be careful," I said. "You got yourself caught up in that crystal—self-hypnosis, I'd say, but I'm not a doctor. Has that ever happened to you before?"

"How strange," she murmured, more to herself than to me. She shook her head again, then looked me in the eye. "When I picked it up, sir, I'd swear something reached out to me! It was so . . . disturbing. Like it wanted to tell me something, but couldn't quite find the strength."

"You must have a vivid imagination," I told her, grinning. "But, just to be safe, how about seeing the auto-doc when you get off duty. Oh, and don't look too closely at those jewels. Okay?"

She nodded, still grave. "Yes, sir." Then she brightened. "Do you have time for a tour of my section of the project, sir?"

I found myself yawning. I'd been up too long. Shaking my head, I said, "No, not now—but definitely later. I've got to rest or I'll be dead on my feet."

She seemed to understand. "Aye, Captain. It's been a busy day."

I headed for my cabin. Laying down in my bed, I closed my eyes and, in seconds, I was deeply asleep.

The next thing I knew, alarm bells were ringing and a loud voice kept calling my name.

Cursing, I somehow managed to get to my feet and stagger over to the intercom. I pounded on the answer button.

"What the hell's going on?" I demanded. "And don't you ever sleep?"

Shucel's face was on the monitor. She seemed strangely pale. "Sir—there's some sort of armed rebellion going on amidship. It seems to be centered around the fusion reactor."

I snapped wide awake, my heart lurching. Every captain's nightmare! "What about the guards?"

"They've moved in—"

"And? And? Come on, I haven't got all day!"

"And—well—they seem to have joined the rebellion. But, sir, it's like nothing I've ever seen before!"

"Damn. Well, put it on my monitor!"

"Yes, sir."

Her face disappeared. The picture of a plain corridor flashed on the screen a second later—and in the corridor moved a pack of my crewmen. At least I thought they were my crewmen. I wouldn't have recognized them if they hadn't been wearing uniforms. Their eyes were strangely white and empty. Sheets of blue electricity crackled over their bodies. I saw a half-dozen guards, several processing techs, maintenance men—people from every part of the ship. And they held, before them, like some sort of holy relics, those blazing star-like crystals they'd made from the first batch of hydrogen skimmed from Aldema Proxima's atmosphere.

My mind went to Tech Friesner's weird hypnotic trance, and suddenly I had one of those rare flashes of insight that occur to us during emergencies. I knew more certainly than I'd ever known anything before that the crystals were, somehow, taking control of my crew's minds. What Jol Mellawithe said came back to me: "Stars are their worlds." It suddenly made perfect sense—perhaps *all* these stars were inhabited by some race or another! And if the native race were hostile. . . .

"Have our people withdraw, if they can," I ordered. "Seal the bulkheads to keep the . . . rebellion isolated."

"What about you, Captain?" she asked anxiously. "You're in occupied territory!"

"Can't you see? This isn't a rebellion! It's an infestation! The crystals have taken control of those crewmen. You must isolate this part of the ship before the contamination spreads. Do it now!"

"Aye, sir." She turned away for a second and I heard her reluctantly passing on my orders. "What else, Captain?"

"Don't worry about me. If anyone can come with an answer, it's going to be Luathek. I'll find him."

"Yes, sir," she said. She started to speak, but I shut off the intercom before she could add anything.

I'd heard a noise outside my room—a strange, half-choked cry, like that of some animal in pain. Running over to my door, I looked through the spy monitor and examined the corridor outside.

Two blank-eyed women were out there. They wore blue uniforms with the gold double-helix sewn on the sleves. Both shuffled toward my cabin, checking the rooms to either side of the hall as they went. Since it wasn't the custom to lock cabin doors on Free Trader vessels, they met no resistance.

I drew a deep breath. Then, throwing open my door, I bolted for the far end of the hall. The women saw me and let out that half-choked hunting cry again, and I couldn't help but shiver. Risking a glance over my shoulder, I noticed with relief that they didn't seem to be able to run. Their best speed was a shambling walk, as if whatever controlled them hadn't yet learned how to work their voluntary muscles.

Reaching an access ladder to the next level, I began to climb without a moment's hesitation. Above me appeared the grid of the next deck's floor. Cautiously, I raised it and peeked out. The corridor was deserted. I paused for a moment, listening, but heard only the soft whir of the air filtration system. Pushing the grid up the rest of the way, I climbed out, then put it back in place.

Through the grillwork, I could see the two possessed women on the deck below. They tried to climb up the ladder, but kept slipping off—they didn't have the coordination necessary for climbing, either. I suspected they couldn't use any intricate movements. Perhaps that could be used as a defense against them. . . .

I turned to the right and ran forward, heading for the laboratory. If the possessed crewmen hadn't reached this level yet, I hoped to find Luathek still safe and sane and hard at work on some pet project. His only hobby, as far as I'd ever been able to find out, was rewiring small tools that worked all right to begin with.

When I reached the lab, I paused just outside the door, listening. I could hear a cheerful humming sound coming from inside—Luathek! Then I swung the door open and ran it.

"Kel!" the Pavian said, eyestalks writhing happily. "What is bringing you here so late?"

"Listen carefully," I said. "We haven't got much time. Those crystals we've been making from the fringe atmosphere of Aldema Proxima—they've got some kind of sentience in them, some esper power. They're taking control of people's minds, and the infection is spreading. We've got to stop them before the whole ship's taken over!"

"Is this a joke?" he asked. "I fail to perceive the humor—"

"No!" I grabbed him and shook him as hard as I could. "Listen to me, Luathek—I'm telling the truth. It's not a joke!"

"Yes . . . yes, Kel. I feel your emotions quite strongly. But it is all so unbelievable to me—"

"Never mind that now! We're running out of time. As far as I can tell, all the lower decks are already infected. I got here just ahead of them. Think! What can we possibly do to stop them?"

"The answer," he said, "would seem obvious—we must destroy the crystals."

"How?"

"There are many ways. Heat . . . acid . . . sound. . . ."

"Sound? What sort of sound?"

"Something to set up a sympathetic vibration in the crystals, something which will then shatter their internal structure, hence destroying the pattern inside them—like a crystal goblet shattering when a singer reaches a certain note—"

"Yes!" I said hurriedly. "That's what we need, but can you do it? How will you find the right frequency to set up the sympathetic vibration?"

"A ranging modular sound set to a half-dozen different frequencies at once should work, Kel. There is equipment of that sort here. It is most useful in repairing communication devices. I can still remember the time on Vinge's World when I had to—"

"Hurry!" I shouted. We didn't have time to listen to his wandering reminiscences.

"Right!" He reached for his tools.

"I'll watch the door," I said.

Within an hour he'd assembled a strange box full of wires and circuit boards, speakers, and all manner of bizarre little bits of equipment I could scarcely begin to identify. His eyestalks writhed with impatience as he made some final adjustment.

Then I saw them outside—a pair of uniformed guards. When they turned toward me and I gazed straight into their perfectly white eyes, I felt a jolt of fear run through me. I backed toward the Pavian.

"Luathek!" I called. "They're coming! Hurry up—the lab door doesn't have a lock!"

"I am almost finished, Kel." Then he stood and closed the box's back panel with an audible snap. "Done."

The lab door burst open and the two guards stood there, eyes glowing white, blue electricity shimmering over their skins. Before them they held the jewels, both of which shone with a brilliant, internal light.

They shambled forward, as though the jewels were drawing them on, dragging them ahead toward us.

"Use the thing!" I shouted at Luathek.

The Pavian moved toward the rear wall, clutching the control box in his four-fingered hand. I scrambled after him, trying to keep as much room between the guards and me as I could. The Pavian pushed the box's button—and nothing happened.

I stared at him. He stared back at me. The guards shambled closer. I began to tremble. "Don't let them touch you with the jewels!" I warned Luathek. "That must be how they're spreading the infestation!"

Grabbing a chair, I threw it at the closest guard. It struck him in the head and bounced off, but didn't slow him down for a second. I tried another. Same reaction.

Turning, I ran to my left, deeper into the lab, and Luathek followed on my heels. Behind us, I heard the possessed men moving to follow, but we easily out-distanced them. At last we reached some sort of storage area, bright blue and red plastic crates had been stacked to the ceiling all around us.

"This way," Luathek said, taking the lead. "There is a cargo lift."

I saw it—a large, railed, box-like structure half-hidden behind a huge pile of oxygen tubes. We pounded around the tubes, leaped over the lift's rails, and jabbed the Up button. The guards were still coming, but they were a good thirty meters behind us.

Immediately, the lift rose. Relaxing a bit, I stood shaking and gasping for breath. By then, we were a good five meters into the air and already out of reach of those below. And then I had a terrible thought: what if more of them were waiting for us above—wherever above was?

"Please be more at ease, Kel," Luathek whispered. He'd caught my fear. "The lift is leading to the ship's hospital. There we will be safe, I think, for a time."

Steel walls rose around us, then an opening appeared and, looking out, I saw the familiar clutter of medical equipment. The place seemed deserted—even Jol Mella-withe had vanished.

Pushing up the guard railing, I walked forward. Only then did I see the damage. The possessed crewmen had already been here. One of the healing tubes had been crushed, and the oily remains of auto-nurses were scattered over the floor. The auto-doctor had been broken into a thousand pieces.

I crossed to the door—and discovered it couldn't be sealed. The ship's engineers hadn't thought to put a lock on the hospital. And, suddenly, a low, choked cry came from the hall outside, followed by another, then another. The sounds grew louder. The creatures were aware of us!

They'd followed our progress through the ship! I hesitated for a second, then smashed in the door's handpad with my elbow. Sparks jumped and something made a sizzling noise, but the door didn't open—and I hoped it would stay that way, at least for the time being.

Luathek opened the control box's back panel, then fiddled with a circuit board. "There!" he said.

All around us, I could hear them moving now. They seemed to be in the air ducts, crawling through the ventilation shafts between the walls. And I knew the ones in the hall were getting closer.

We were trapped.

"Will it work?" I whispered.

"I am so thinking, Kel." Luathek hesitated a second, then pushed the single red button on the top of the box. I heard a low humming sound—then nothing. It wasn't working. They'd be on us in seconds!

"Hurry!" I whispered.

He tore off the back panel, then took a sonic screwdriver from the tool pouch at his side. As he probed the box's innards, I heard a scratching sound behind me. When I turned, I saw the door's blue plastic had begun to glow red-orange around its edges. A trickle of noxious black smoke rose.

"Ah!" Luathek said. "Here is the problem—a bad connection!" He put the screwdriver away and slipped the back of the box into place again. "I can sense them outside. Their emotions are clear to me. They will soon break through the door. Perhaps I should try to communicate with them? It might be possible—"

The door shuddered. I heard fists pounding on it. "There's no time!" I said. "Hurry!"

"Now I should activate the device?"

"Yes!" I screamed.

He pushed the button.

For an instant, nothing happened. I had a terrible feeling in the pit of my stomach. Then I heard the low hum— and it slowly rose in volume, becoming a bone-grating roar of sound. I covered my ears. Setting the box on the floor, Luathek did the same. I looked at him and grinned, nodding so he understood how ecstatic I was, even though I was in excruciating pain. Luathek's eyestalks were pressed close to his head, but he, too, nodded. If it worked, we'd won!

I could no longer hear the possessed crewmen outside— the hum was now so loud I could scarcely think—but I pressed the broken pad until the door slowly dilated. Whatever they'd been using to try to melt it must've damaged the opening mechanism, I realized.

A half-dozen uniformed guards lay on the deck, gems clutched in their hands. The crystals no longer gleamed brightly, and several had developed visible flaws—cracks in their centers, or dark blemishes on their facets. Whatever presence had occupied them had certainly been destroyed. Perhaps they wouldn't be worth so much money now . . . but that no longer mattered! At least, not to me.

My men began waking up. They groaned and rubbed their heads. But they seemed to be themselves again.

"Calmen? Sorth? Bushyager?" I asked, reading their names off their breast pockets. "How do you feel?"

"My head aches," Sorth said. He clutched the double-helix medallion around his neck as though drawing strength from it. Rubbing his eyes, he stood. The others echoed his words.

"What do you remember of the last few hours?" I demanded.

"Just . . . we were trying to stop some sort of mutiny. . . .

They were all around us, and suddenly someone hit
me—"

"They took over your mind through the crystals," I
said. "Luathek and I found something to stop them at the
last minute. Now we've got to retake the rest of the ship.
Luathek!"

He picked up the box and hurried out. "Yes, Kel?"

"What's the range of that sound machine of yours?"

"Effectively—perhaps thirty meters. Beyond that I hold
many uncertainties."

"Can you hook it into the ship's intercom so it can be
heard all over the ship at once?"

"Yes, Kel. That should be most easy from the control
room."

"Then we'll start there. Guards, draw your guns and
fall in around us. Remember, if anything happens to
Luathek or that box, we're dead!"

"Yes, sir!"

We headed for the lift. The wailing noise of the box
spread around us, penetrating into the cabins. By the time
we reached the lift, we'd added fifteen crewmen to our
band of rescued mutineers and fifteen now-flawed jewels to
our "captured" list.

When we reached the sealed bulkhead dividing the ship
into two (our party now numbering twenty-odd), I called
Shucel Baref on the intercom.

"Captain! How do I know that's you?" she said before I
could speak.

"Who else would it be? And—as you can see—I've
accomplished what I said I would. Luathek and I have a
way to stop the spread of the creatures. You can hear the
humming, I trust?"

"Yes, sir?" She sounded doubtful.

"It shatters the crystals. Now let us through. We need to

---

use the ship's intercom to broadcast the sound through the ship."

She hesitated.

"Do it!" I said.

"Yes, sir." She turned and I heard her speaking to Jamis.

Then the bulkhead's warning system shrilled and we all stepped back. With a low grinding noise, the steel wall before us pulled up into the ceiling. We continued down the corridor, heading for the lift that would take us to the control room.

It was deceptively easy to recapture the ship—and it took less than ten minutes, not counting the mad scramble to assemble the machine. Luathek floated next to the ship's intercom and I switched it on. The humming sound blared through all the loudspeakers, deafening, mind-numbing, losing none of its power.

Within a minute we were getting puzzled reports from all over the ship. And—on the monitors—we saw only confused, headachy crewmen.

"You've done it, sir!" Jamis said. He was bleary-eyed. I realized he hadn't slept in the last twenty-four hours.

I grinned. "Did you ever have any doubts?"

"Not for a second, sir." He grinned back wearily.

"You're ahead of me then," I said, still remembering my panicked feelings when I thought we were trapped in the laboratory.

Luathek shut off the box's hum. "Is that all for now, Kel?"

"Yes—and a good job, too, Luathek. I'm putting you in for a Special Merit bonus and promotion."

His eyestalks writhed with pride. "Most appreciation," he murmured.

I turned to my intercom and flipped the switch, calling the processing center. In seconds, a bewildered, white-coated technician answered. I didn't recognize him.

"Sir?" he said.

"All work on processing the jewels is hereby ordered stopped," I said. "If another is made, I'll shove the tech who did it into an airlock without a suit, then space him. Is that understood?"

"Sir! I'll see to it at once."

"Make sure that you do." I snapped the intercom off. "Jamis."

"Yes, Captain?"

"I'm declaring a Class One emergency. I want all the crystals found and brought to the forward airlock."

"Right away. Anything else, sir?"

"Yes." I paused. "Find someone to relieve you, and go take a nap."

The clean-up took the rest of the night. All my men returned to their posts (the only damage they seemed to have suffered—except for severe headaches—were bruises from where they'd fallen when the crystals shattered). Jol Mellawithe was found wandering the corridors in a half-drugged state. A new auto-doctor was activated—the old one having been smashed beyond repair—and set about treating him again—but without the orders to keep him sedated.

Ulega Max called me once. He appeared unruffled by the night's events—but then, he and the other Council members slept near the control room, and hadn't been affected by the take-over. His face was a frozen mask as he said, "We wish to speak with you, Captain Corrian, at your earliest convenience."

I nodded. "It will have to be in several hours. There are too many details to take care of."

"I understand. At your convenience." And then the screen went dark.

"Sir," Jamis said. He'd just come back on duty, and now appeared as unruffled as ever. "Perhaps you ought to look at the monitor—a ship's just entered the system."

"Thanks." I ordered the computer to bring up the hologram of the system. The air in front of me shimmered, then grew dark. A tapestry of stars appeared—and against them a long, needle-like shape moved. The image's resolution grew greater as the scans took in more detail. Gun turrets bristled along the newcomer's sides, and two small shuttleports broadened the stern with their rounded docking bays.

It was a Scoutship—the Patrol used such craft.

"They're broadcasting their registration codes, sir," Shucel said. "It's the *S. P. Somtow*—a Patrol ship. The captain wishes to speak to you."

"Put him on my private viewscreen."

"Aye, sir." Her fingers flew over the controls.

The small screen on the arm of my chair flickered with black and white lines for an instant, then a picture appeared: that of a small, gray-skinned human of obvious Barnard Star ancestry. He wore not only the blue and gold uniform of a Patrol captain, but the characteristic sneer that went along with it.

I took an instant dislike to the man.

"Well, Captain"—he began, then glanced down at something off the monitor—"Corrian. My name is Felwoon Ipijar. Commander Ipijar. You are hereby ordered to stop all activity and prepare to be boarded. Your ship's equipment is being confiscated."

"What?" I demanded, hardly able to believe what I'd heard. "What?"

"You heard me, Corrian. Con-fi-sca-ted. It's an easy

enough word to understand. Look it up in your computer's lexicon. If that old scow you command even has a computer."

"Why, you're nothing but a pirate, you—"

"You'd better watch what you say, Corrian." He leaned forward, oozing smugness. "I'd hate to think what would happen to you if you didn't cooperate with me. The Patrol doesn't take kindly to smugglers like you and your crew. We've received a full report on your drug-running operation."

"But—" I started.

He cut me off. "I know your kind. I know you'll cooperate with me to your fullest. After all, you'll just buy-off the judge and never face a prison term. Prepare to receive my soldiers. We're taking over the *Marrow Falcon* until further notice." Then the screen flickered with static.

I swallowed hard, anger and fear fighting for control. Smugglers, indeed! The charge was utterly ridiculous. And how could he have possibly received a report on us when we were so far from any established trade routes?

Suddenly, I wondered if he really was a Patrol captain. A ship's registration codes could be forged. An old Patrol Scoutship could've been reconditioned. If he turned out to be a pirate . . . if he came aboard and seized the starskimming equipment . . .

I thought of the *Marrow Falcon*'s Blackmark-model shuttles, thought of what they could do against a small Scoutship like Ipijar's. He wouldn't last five minutes against us. . . .

Reluctantly, I put my hot-headed thoughts aside and made the decision to surrender to Ipijar. I didn't dare take the chance of firing on a Patrol ship. We've done nothing wrong, after all. Whatever they want us for has to be a mistake. It'll be straightened out in time. If not, I'll file a formal complaint. *Turn to page 126.*

I'll fight! That bastard can't be from the Patrol. He's obviously up to no good. I have to protect the starskimming equipment. It's too valuable to take a chance of having it stolen. *Turn to page 117.*

THE LAST BATTLE

I decided to fight back, to try and scare them off. All we needed, I thought, was a show of force to keep them at a safe distance. After all, I couldn't let aliens attack my ship and get away with it. If I did, they'd feel free to attack again and again whenever they felt like it, and they'd have no fears about doing so. Next time, someone might get seriously hurt.

"And after the shuttles get back," I said, "we're going to prepare to counter attack . . . fire a few energy weapons near enough for them to feel the blast, but not near enough they'll get hurt."

"But, Captain—" Shucel started. Then she looked away.

"What?" I said.

"Captain . . . they invaded our ship. That's enough of a declaration of war!"

"Have you forgotten that we entered this system without their knowledge? That we've skimmed their sun without permission? Try and look at things from their point of view."

"Yes, sir. I . . . I see you're right." She turned back to her work.

"Captain Corrian!"

Turning, I saw Ulega Max floating in the doorway. He pulled himself toward my command seat. I pushed myself away from the wall and drifted toward the center of the room to meet him. The techs had the computer working, and, when I sat, I saw its information screen flickering at the edge of perception. I felt better having it there.

Rubbing my eyes, I asked, "Yes, Ulega?"

"I have a message from the Ship's Council."

"What is it?"

"You are to attack the aliens and drive them back to Xel-thufed. Our starskimming must go on as scheduled."

I hesitated. I could, of course, veto the action since it was a combat situation . . . but what Ulega wanted wasn't so hard. I could make the show of force a bit more flashy to impress him. Perhaps firing energy bolts into Xelthufed itself would be a good idea. . . .

At last I nodded. "As you request."

"Good. See to it at once." He turned and pulled himself toward the door.

I leaned back to activate the computer, and it answered at once.

"Yes, Captain Corrian?"

"Prepare a detailed analysis of the star-creatures' attack," I said.

"Already prepared, Captain Corrian, per system orders. The aliens' attack took the form of highly ordered electric and magnetic interference which most of the ship's equipment was unable to absorb or deflect."

"Interesting. Suggestions for a counter attack?"

"Nuclear disruptions have been known to affect ordered electrical and magnetic fields, Captain Corrian."

"Would the Blackmark-model shuttles be able to provide such a nuclear disruption with weapons already aboard?"

"Yes, Captain Corrian."

I smiled. "Good." Already a plan had begun to form in the back of my mind: a couple of systematic strikes from nullspace with the shuttles—quick strafing runs on Xel-thufed's atmosphere to stir things up there, a couple of atomic explosions in space, several kilometers from the star-creatures we could see. Nothing too impressive, just enough to give them all headaches they wouldn't soon forget. The star-creatures sitting between the *Falcon* and Xel-thufed would be forced to return to their star.

"Captain," Jamis said, "the shuttles have been sighted."

"Where?"

"They slipped into realspace about a thousand meters from the aliens, sighted us, then slipped again . . . wait! They just slipped a couple of hundred meters from us, sir. They're moving toward the transport tubes at the sides of the ship."

That meant they'd taken a full load of Xelthufed's atmosphere between them. They'd unload it directly in the fusion reactor room, and there Ulega Max's scientists would work their magic and produce jewels from pure energy.

I touched the intercom and opened communications with Commander Omm's ship. She appeared on the viewscreen at once.

"Yes, Captain?" she said.

"We've been attacked," I said, "by aliens living inside the star. The ship's on alert. Unload your cargo, then prepare for new orders."

She stiffened noticeably, but saluted and signed off without a word of protest or even a request for more information. She was the ideal commander to lead the attack, I decided then and there. I knew she'd do exactly as instructed without argument.

"Computer," I said.

"Yes, Captain Corrian?"

"Put up the holograph of the shuttles' unloading."

"Yes, Captain Corrian."

Immediately, the picture leaped into view in front of me. The shuttles stood perhaps twenty meters apart and had a funnel-shaped force shield stretching from a place directly between them to a transport tube in the *Falcon*'s side. Brilliantly colored gases, swirling a bit, poured from the ships' holds into the funnel, down into the bowels of the *Marrow Falcon*.

As I watched, intrigued, the intercom beeped softly.

"Yes?" I said.

"Kel, it is Luathek speaking at you. I wish to make my report of damages now."

"Go ahead."

"Aside from a few fires which fused wiring, there is no physical damage. Various automatic breaker switches flipped to prevent injury to the equipment, and that is what caused all the darknesses and computer black-outs throughout the ship."

"What about the explosion we heard?"

"That was the noise of the midship bulkhead sealing itself to prevent loss of internal atmosphere in case the hull was breached. It has since been re-opened."

"Fix the fused wiring, then report to me again. If anything else needs to be fixed, take care of it, too. I want the *Falcon* fighting-fit as soon as possible."

"Yes, Kel. The wiring's repair will take less than an hour." The intercom clicked and he was gone.

The shuttles finished unloading their cargo of superheated gases skimmed from Xelthufed's fringe atmosphere. As the force shields collapsed, the ships moved toward the docking cradles at either end of the *Falcon*. There they would be refueled.

I wasn't going to launch the shuttles again until the *Falcon* was fully prepared. Luathek had said it would take less than an hour.

I began to count the minutes.

"Launch the shuttles," I said.

The holograph in the center of the room showed all four shuttles leaving their cradles. Their thrusters left a trail of mist that reflected Xelthufed's light in a tiny rainbow for a second before the ice particles scattered too far for the human eye to follow. I could hear Omm's voice issuing commands over the intercom. The other shuttles fell into position, applying thrusters gently as they moved away from the *Falcon*. They banded together into a tight diamond-shaped formation—the best formation for strafing runs from space.

The ships seemed to ripple as force shields went up around them. Then, like a curtain being pulled across their diamond formation, they vanished from sight— slipped into nullspace and the ether currents.

There was nothing else I could do except wait.

The shuttles appeared on the holograph of the star one after another, energy guns blazing away into Xelthufed's atmosphere. For a brief moment, it seemed to me that the star burned brighter—and then the shuttles were gone, slipped back into nullspace, circling around and preparing for another attack run. But had their bombardment worked? What sort of disruption had it done to the aliens' population, their cities, their world? I would never know. But I hoped—

"Sir," Jamis cried. "The star-creatures—they're leaving!"

"Which ones?"

"All of them that attacked us. They're heading toward Xelthufed at almost half the speed of light!"

"Then the attacks were successful," I said coolly. "We got a reaction." But what if they've only gone to get reinforcements? I asked myself, feeling more apprehensive than I let on.

"Prepare for nullspace slip," I said.

They all stared at me. "Sir?" several said. One even dared ask, "But what about the shuttles, sir?"

"I haven't forgotten them!" I snapped. "And I'm not used to having my orders questioned! Set up the calculations for a nullspace slip or I'll have you all relieved of duty!"

They set about the task—a bit sullenly, it seemed to me. I knew I'd have to discipline them later. I couldn't have them questioning my every command. I hadn't forgotten the shuttles. I merely wanted more room between us and Xelthufed. The shuttles would catch up with little trouble.

"Sir," Jamis said, "there's trouble at the fusion reactor."

"What sort of trouble?" I asked. Something made me uneasy—a sudden, strange premonition. I had visions of the jewel processing equipment running amok, spewing super-heated hydrogen throughout the ship.

"I'm not sure, sir," he said hesitantly. "The reports aren't clear—it seems one of the refinery techs seized a guard's gun and went berserk. More guards have been called to restrain him."

I looked down and saw that, indeed, a red alarm light was blinking close to my right elbow. I hadn't noticed it in the excitement. If it was just a security problem, it would wait. "I can't take time to deal with it now," I said. "Order Security to keep me posted. They can take care of the matter. I'll see to that tech later."

"Yes, sir," he said. He turned back to the communications net monitor and I could hear him speaking softly to Security.

The shuttles shot the star twice more, then withdrew into nullspace, maneuvering to return to the *Marrow Falcon*.

As I leaned back, satisfied, Jamis called to me. His face

was white. "Armed rebellion amidships, sir," he cried, his voice cracking. "The reports—they're garbled, but it seems the refinery techs have banded together. Something about jewels . . . I don't understand it. Security is on the line. What should I tell them? Do you want to talk to them?"

I sighed. "Yes. I'll take care of it."

Touching the viewscreen controls, I reached Security's main office in less than a second. The young, red-headed guard on duty leaped to his feet when he saw my face on the monitor, snapping a quick salute. His uniform was spotless—I guessed he was on his first assignment on the *Falcon*.

"Captain, sir!"

"Never mind that," I snapped. "Who's in charge there?"

"Me, sir! First Guard Molx just—uh—stepped out, sir."

"What do you mean, 'stepped out'? Stepped out where?"

"He went to C-Section, sir. To try and hold back the refinery techs. I can see them on the corridor monitor, sir— They're driving the guards back! They'll be here in minutes, sir! What should I do? Sir! What should I do?"

"Stay there," I said. My fingers fairly danced over the controls as I flipped through pictures from the thousand-odd monitors scattered through the ship. I finally found the view the young guard saw. The sight frightened me more than I could say.

I looked down a long, straight corridor. Guards crouched at the near end, their backs toward the monitor, as they fired shot after shot at the slowly advancing men. There was a good deal of smoke and steam from melted wall panels. But through the smoke I could still see the men advancing. Slowly, awkwardly, as if the feel of their bodies was strange to them.

The refinery techs.

Blue electricity crackled over their bodies, and in their hands they held what looked like miniature suns . . . the jewels they had been making. Energy bolts hit them in the face and seemed to dissipate, or struck their crackling blue halos and deflected harmlessly to either side. Their eyes seemed oddly vacant, as though no human intelligence moved them, but something else, something both alien and sinister.

The jewels! Somehow they'd taken control of my men! How? Why?

I shuddered, suddenly cold.

The guards fell back. I flipped through the monitors until I found them again in a corridor exactly like the last one. The techs marched inexorably onward.

The intercom crackled with static.

"Captain," a hoarse voice said. "First Guard Molx here."

I punched the button. "Yes. I see you on the monitor."

"We—we can't stop them, sir! Nothing works! I want to bring up heavier arms. I need your word now."

"Do it!"

Static snapped over the intercom—he was gone.

Looking up, I beckoned to the guard by the door to my side. "You, there! Where're the control room's weapons kept?"

"Down the hall, in the storage room, sir."

"Get enough for everybody here," I ordered.

The guard turned and pulled himself toward the door as fast as he could. Jamis, too, had been watching the monitors.

"Captain," he reported, "the control room where the

Ship's Council lives can be sealed off from the rest of the ship. It can be launched as an escape vessel."

"I know it can," I said. "The situation's not that desperate yet."

The guards on the monitor were making one last effort to dig in and stop the techs' advance. They were hauling up heavier guns—ones strong enough to blow a hole in the ship's hull, if their enerby bolts were loosed in the wrong direction.

It was then that I saw Luathek among the techs. His eyestalks were held listlessly, and blue electricity flickered over his body. In his hands, he held a pair of jewels.

They'd gotten to him. There was a burning in my stomach, and my head hurt. My eyes ached from staring at his image and willing him away, willing him back to his post and safety, willing him out of danger. How could they have done this to my best friend? I almost cried with the pain.

And, to make things worse, I knew he'd been the crew member most likely to come up with a way to stop the attack. Intelligent, creative—everything we needed in this situation. But now it was too late. Somehow he'd fallen victim to the attackers' power.

And now the guards were aiming the energy cannon straight toward him. I tried to call an order for them to stop, that it was Luathek—but I was too late.

A blinding white light filled the viewscreen. For an instant, I thought the monitor had gone dead. And then, through a haze of smoke and fire, I saw the cannon hadn't had any effect! The techs and Luathek still advanced, their bodies whole and unblemished despite the searing heat that must've swept over them only seconds before.

I swallowed. How could anything have lived through that cannon blast?

Then the techs were on top of the guards, pinning them

down. The sounds of screaming men filled my ears. The noise wrenched at my gut. I stood up, yelling at them to fall back, to get away—

A pale, four-fingered, Pavian hand reached up toward the viewscreen . . . and the monitor went dead.

As I collapsed back into my seat, I found myself covered with cold sweat. My hands shook. My stomach ached with a dull pain. My head pounded and I could hear my heart beating too loud, too fast.

The door dilated and Jol Mellawithe burst in. His hair swung wildly about his head and his gray suit was ripped and stained by blood. He saw me and tried to pull himself over, but the guard grabbed his arm and held him back.

"Let go of me!" he shouted. He tried to wrench free, but couldn't.

"Let him go," I yelled.

The guard looked at me in surprise, but obeyed at once. Jol shot from his grasp and spun toward me. He managed to grab the edge of my command chair and pull himself to a stop.

"Captain—" he gasped. "You've got to stop them!"

"Who?"

"The star-creatures!"

I frowned. "I've got a rebellion on my hands. I haven't got time to worry about aliens."

"Don't you see, sir?" he cried. "The aliens are the one taking control of your crewmen through the jewels!"

I stared at him, shocked. It all came together, suddenly—the tech in the refinery going berserk, the crewmen carrying the jewels, the guards being unable to stop them. It was like a fire spreading through the ship, destroying everything it touched.

"How can I stop them?"

"I . . . I don't know, sir."

A ringing filled my ears. I didn't know what to do. In all my training, nothing had prepared me for this. No wonder the aliens had returned to their sun without a fight. They had their own people already on board, capturing us from within.

I went over it and over it in my mind, thinking up the wildest schemes—and rejecting all of them. I wanted to crawl into a hole and pull the entrance in over me. There was nothing left for me. Nothing but the final duty any captain faces: to destroy my ship rather than let it fall into enemy hands.

The twelve techs in the room were staring at me.

"We're lost," I told them. "You saw. Nothing can stop them."

"Sir . . . ." Jamis said softly.

"You all saw what they were like. The ship's armaments can't fall into their hands. I must see to the ship's destruction." My voice broke. I knew that if I left here, I might soon fall prey to the possessed techs. I'd be dead at their hands—or worse.

I finally realized what had happened. The star-creatures had been defending themselves when they attacked. The shuttles had skimmed up not only Xelthufed's atmosphere but star-creatures too. Now they were trapped in those jewels, exerting their will and power on my crew. And I was helpless to stop them.

I had nothing left to lose. My ship was gone. My best friend was gone. I would never hold command again. I could only have one last moment of dignity.

I straightened up, trying to sound confident. "As soon as I leave," I said, "warn the Ship's Council to evacuate. Then, seal the command center and launch yourselves into space. Get to the nearest Patrol base and tell them what happened. Get this system quarantined—it's the last hope.

I name Tech Shucel Baref as acting captain."

"Yes, sir," Shucel whispered, looking very pale and afraid. I'd given her authority over all that was left of the ship. Now I hoped she could stand the pressure.

I grabbed the nearest rung and pulled myself toward the door. A numbness had settled in. My mind seemed to have wandered from its ties to my body.

Just as I reached for the handpad, the door opened. The outside guard stood there. I pulled him in, took one of the handguns he held, and left. Behind me, I could hear thick steel panels dropping into place, shutting the control center off from the rest of the ship. The process would take a few minutes. I'd be well clear of the area by then— hopefully in the arms room. I'd do as much damage to the hand weapons as I could, then blow a hole in the hull with an energy cannon, destroying everything.

I hoped.

The last deed of a doomed commander. . . .

Cautiously, I made my way down the corridor, keeping my footsteps as soft and quiet as I could. At each intersection I paused for a second, listening, then continued if I heard nothing.

Then, finally, at a tube-lift I heard them. They had spread out and seemed to be searching the ship in an orderly manner.

I retreated, padding down a corridor that seemed to grow longer before me. Risking a glance back over my shoulder, I saw them fifty meters behind. And they saw me. They shuffled forward, and an alarm seemed to go up among them, for they poured into the corridor by the dozens—all the techs, all the guards, all the crew of the *Falcon*. They all held brightly shining jewels. Blue electricity crackled over their bodies, marking them as no longer human.

I darted to the right—and almost ran into Luathek and four guards. The Pavian stepped forward slowly, ponderously, and raised a jewel to try and touch my face. Leaping back, I dropped my handgun, and narrowly avoided him. Then, scrambling to my feet, I fled.

I was in the main corridor and running again, but by now I was completely turned around, lost.

I reached a dead end and there was nowhere left to go but into the small cabin to my right. I darted in and sealed the door shut, switching the handpad to Lock.

Within minutes I heard them outside, scratching like dogs wanting in. The metal door started to glow blue around the edges and the paint flaked away, as if some unimaginable force were being exerted on it. They'd be inside in a second, on top of me, touching me with their jewels, making me like them.

I sat quietly and waited, weeping for what might have been.

THE END

PATROL SPY

I decided to try and negotiate with the star-creatures. It's an historically proven fact that most wars between different species are caused by simple misunderstandings. Figuring a misunderstanding had to be at fault here, I concluded that the best way to get work going again would be to contact the aliens (if possible) and explain to them what we were doing. Perhaps our negotiations would even lead to the star-creatures joining the League, with all the trade and other privileges that go along with membership.

"After that," I told Shucel, "we'll contact the star-creatures and see if we can get some sort of treaty with them that will allow us to skim the star."

I didn't add: If we manage, somehow, to communicate with them.

"Yes, sir," she said, her voice carefully expressionless as she went back to her station. She obviously thought I was crazy. I wondered about that myself.

Perhaps the scientist, Jol Mellawithe, would be able to figure something out, I thought suddenly. Certainly, he'd detected the aliens' communication system when nobody else could. . . .

I called Security on the intercom. The small viewscreen set into the arm of the command chair flickered briefly, then the image appeared: that of a young, dark-haired woman dressed in a red and black Second Guard's uniform. She straightened when she saw me, snapping a hasty salute.

"Captain, sir!"

"Security is holding a scientist, Jol Mellawithe. I want him released and escorted here at once."

"Yes, sir!"

"Get to it. You have five minutes." I switched off the viewscreen.

Mellawithe was at my side in three and a half. He looked a bit paler than before, but otherwise seemed in fine health . . . which caused me to wonder if his wild accusations about Ulega Max drugging him before might not be true. Waving the guards away, I stood and escorted him out into the hall.

"I owe you an apology," I said when we were alone.

"That's all right, Captain," he said, flushing. "I understand your position completely. I must've seemed insane when I called you—"

"That's behind us now, sir," We reached a lift and I summoned a tube-car. "You know about the attack, I assume."

"It was hard to miss, sir."

"Well, I'm going to need your help." The tube-car came and we got in. The doors hissed shut when I keyed in our destination, then we started forward.

"The star-creatures didn't do any real damage to the ship," I continued, "but I need to know why they attacked when the starskimming began. Will it happen every time the shuttles skim, or was it something else? In short, I need a way to communicate with them. Since you're the only one who's got any ideas on the subject, you're in charge of the project. Any ideas?"

The tube stopped. "Yes, sir," he said, his face lighting up eagerly. "To start with, I think I know why the aliens attacked the ship." The doors opened and we got out at a small, bare room with a guard on duty at the far end.

"Why?"

"I think it's obvious, sir. The shuttles not only got Xel-thufed's atmosphere, they skimmed up several of the star-creatures."

I stopped short. "I never thought of that!"

"No? Well, mark it down to the military mind-set, begging your pardon, sir. Starship captains throughout history have always been blind to what's obvious to a scientist. The opposite is true as well, sadly."

We entered the next room—a huge, circular, sprawling laboratory. Equipment gleamed with polish. Small lights blinked in odd patterns. Men and women in sanitary white and blue uniforms moved about from machine to machine, running tests, doing whatever needed to be done in preparation for refining the star's atmosphere into jewels. They all wore the ever-present double-helix symbolizing Ghu, as though this symbol represented their god, looking down, protecting them and their work.

One by one they stood aside as they noticed me. Several cast startled glances at Jol Mellawithe, but their faces settled into unreadable masks.

"The shuttles will not be unloading their cargo," I said, "due to the problems we've had with the star-creatures. I have a new job for you in the meantime, though—you're going to do whatever Jol Mellawithe tells you to do. I want to be able to communicate with the aliens within a day." There were startled, angry murmurs. The undercurrent of noise dropped off, however, as I clapped Jol on the shoulder. "Get to it."

That reminded me of the spectroscopic analysis of the star that I'd ordered the computer to make. I crossed to the nearest computer, put in my access code, then called up the data.

It scrolled across the screen, pages and pages of text.

Mellawithe grinned. "I already have all that, sir," he said.

Shrugging, I said, "It keeps the computer off the streets at night."

When I returned to the control room, I expected the shuttles to have already arrived. Strangely, they hadn't. I began to wonder whether the star-creatures had chased them into nullspace and wrecked them there. It was a frightening possibility. I shook my head. No, they were a little late, that was all—nothing to worry about yet. But still. . . .

"Captain," Jamis reported, "I have the shuttles on my screen."

I relaxed. "Where?"

"They slipped into realspace about a thousand meters from the star-creatures, sighted us, then slipped again. Wait a second—they just slipped into realspace several hundred meters from us. They're moving toward the transport tubes, sir."

I relaxed. They'd made it through all right. They must've taken a full load of Xelthufed's atmosphere between them without any trouble. If Mellawithe was right and they had scooped up a number of aliens by accident, I certainly couldn't let the creatures be set loose in the ship. I called Commander Omm up on the viewscreen.

"Yes, Captain?" she said.

"You are not to unload your cargo," I said. "We've been attacked by aliens living in the star. You may have accidentally captured some of them. Until we know for sure, we can't do anything with your cargo. I want you to take it back and dump it into the star."

"An attack? What happened, sir?"

"No damage," I said as reassuringly as possible. "It was just a show of force . . . a sample of their power, I suppose. I have no intention of fighting a war here. Take the shuttles' cargo back at once."

"Yes, Captain. We'll start plotting the return course

immediately, sir."

The viewscreen went dark.

An instant later, it flickered back to life and I found myself looking at Ulega Max's face.

"What can I do for you, Ulega?" I said.

"Come to the conference room at once. That's an order."

With a reluctant sigh, I said, "I'll be there in a minute." Ulega Max had definitely begun to get on my nerves.

The screen went dark. "Keep things going smoothly," I told Shucel. "I want to be paged if the aliens make a move."

"Yes, sir," she said. "No problem."

I headed for the conference room.

"No! No! No!" Ulega Max shouted. "You are to call those shuttles back!" His face was a deep red, his nostrils flared, his fists clenched. I'd never seen anyone so angry. "Think of the cost! Think of the lost profits! I demand you order the shuttles to return here and unload their cargo now!"

I shook my head slowly. "Consider carefully what you're saying—if the shuttles did skim up members of the star-creatures' species by accident, this could mean more fighting. They attacked us once. It was a show of strength, nothing more—a sample of what they could do if we don't cooperate. They knocked out all the ship's equipment in minutes! We'd be helpless to stop them if they attacked again. No, I can't risk it.

"We're going to take the situation one step at a time, as slowly as I feel is necessary, and the first step is dumping the atmosphere the shuttles skimmed. You made me captain, and I'm not going to get my ship destroyed because you've got a sudden greed for a higher profit."

His face darkened. "The Council runs the ship. You will do as we say."

"You're no longer in control," I said. "Under the League's laws I'm now in sole command. Section 22, Paragraph 7 of the Interplanetary Code: 'When attacked by hostile forces, all responsibility reverts to the ship's captain for the duration of the emergency.' Do you want me to quote the rest?"

"I knew it was a mistake to hire you," he said softly. Still, I heard the stress in his voice—the mingled anger and frustration. "The others thought we could control you because you were so young and inexperienced. I knew the minute I saw you they were wrong. You're a fool, Kel Corrian. Your contract with us will not be renewed." With that, he turned and stalked away, cape fluttering out behind him.

I watched him go, feeling at once sad and angry and relieved. I had won the confrontation—but, perhaps, at the cost of my job. If I wanted to stay on as the *Falcon*'s captain, I knew I'd better prove my point to the other two Council members. Their votes combined could override Max's.

The rest of the day passed quickly—and yet not much happened. The aliens remained in space between my ship and Xelthufed, not attacking, not doing anything. Jol Mellawithe and the various scientists and techs under him continued work, trying to come up with a device to contact the star-creatures. Ulega Max and the other Council members took great pains to avoid me as I made my rounds of the ship.

At last, when I was in my cabin preparing to file my day's reports with the ship's computer, the intercom beeped. Jol Mellawithe was on the viewscreen. I pushed the button to reply, and his smile broadened when he saw me.

"What's new?" I asked.

"I think we've done it—come up with a way to communicate with the star-creatures, I mean. If you'll come down to the forward workshop, we'll try it out now."

"Thanks," I said. "I'll be there in a minute."

I filed the last report away, then headed for the workshop.

It was a small, gray room located not far from the command center. As I stood in the doorway, I looked over the conglomeration of equipment on the table in the room's center. There were no other furnishings. The electronic equipment was a hodge-podge of dials, lights, tubes, circuitry boards—it looked as if it had been assembled from leftover bits of metal and spare parts. I wasn't terribly impressed with its appearance. I only hoped it did its job.

Jol Mellawithe and Luathek both waited there for me. They smiled smugly, confidently.

"Kel!" the Pavian said, eyestalks writhing with excitement, "I have just completed work on the machine you wanted. It is connected to the ship's communication system. It will transmit coded energy waves to the creatures waiting outside."

"That's right, sir," Jol said. "I'm going to make the first test right now—to see if they'll respond to signals mimicking the ones I picked up when I first discovered their communications net. If we get any response, we'll know we're on the right track and be able to continue work in that direction."

"Excellent," I said. "By all means—proceed!"

He touched the controls gingerly, like a musician trying out a new instrument. I heard nothing but a slight humming noise and frowned doubtfully.

"Is it working?" I asked.

"Yes, yes, sir," Jol said in excitement. "The speaker will transform their response into something the human ear can pick up—provided there is a response."

He stopped and leaned forward, straining to hear. I heard only static then—after a series of snaps and whistles—a low, grating, oddly accented voice that said in Basic, "We have our kill awareness most fully comprehending words our own."

"How— How—" I began. "How can they know Basic?"

"They must've taken it from the computers when they hit the ship, sir," Jol muttered. His fingers played over the keyboard again. "I'm asking them—in Basic—if they mean us harm."

Again came their mystifying reply: "All words kill try going inward thank we enough kill kill."

"I don't understand," I said.

"It's obvious they have the vocabulary for a dialog, but don't know how to put the words together. Don't you see, sir? They've never encountered words before. This is marvelous! Fantastic! Incredible! Think how differently their minds must work!"

"All I care about is that they don't attack us, and that we can get on with the starskimming as quickly and safely as possible. Tell them that."

He shook his head. "Impossible, sir. We haven't reached that point yet. First, we have to be able to understand each other's meaning. Just getting the words in the right order will be an enormous achievement for them. We can't expect them to understand us until we can understand them, too. Do you understand what I mean, Captain?"

"Yes. Do your best—as fast as possible!"

"I'll work on it, sir," Mellawithe said. He turned to

Luathek. "Everything seems to be working. You did an excellent job setting up the equipment. I want to thank you."

"They are nothingnesses," Luathek said, dipping his eyestalks.

"I will assign several high techs from the command center to work with you," I told Jol. "I want to know when you manage to get a dialog going with the star-creatures." I stifled a yawn. "I've been up too long. If I don't get some rest soon, I'll be useless to anyone."

"Don't expect any sudden developments, sir," Jol said, shaking his head. "We were lucky they're intelligent enough to raid the computers and pick up Basic. I can tell talking to them is going to be a linguistic mess. There are two linguists aboard, by the way. I'd like to draft them, with your permission, sir."

"Yes, certainly. If anyone else on board can help, just say so."

"I think that'll take care of everything, sir. Thank you for all you've done."

"I should thank you," I said, stifling a yawn. "You may well have saved the ship—and me along with it!" I nodded once, then turned and headed for my cabin. All the last few days' events were catching up with me. I was suddenly exhausted.

It was late the next day.

No substantial progress had yet been made in communicating with the aliens, and I'd gone to the command center to look over Mellawithe's initial report. The man never slept, it seemed. He'd clearly been working all night.

"Sir," Shucel said, interrupting my thought, "a ship just realspaced into the system!"

"Registry?" I asked, surprised.

"None being broadcast, sir."

"Identify the make."

"Too distant to be certain—but the computer has made a tentative analysis. It's probably a Nemesis Class cruiser, sir, and it's certainly armed. Now it's heading straight for us at full speed."

"Damn." A Nemesis Class cruiser was one of the most awe-inspiring fighting machines every built. It had enough fire-power to devastate the surface of an entire planet from orbit, or to punch so many holes in a ship like the *Marrow Falcon* that she could never be repaired again.

"Signal them," I said, following protocol. "Identify us. Tell them I want to speak to their captain."

"Yes, sir," Jamis said. He turned to his console and broadcast my message. A minute passed, then two. He tried again—with the same result.

"There's no reply, sir."

"Sound Red Alert," I ordered. "Everybody to battle stations. Raise the force shields and prepare for nullspace slip." I planned on taking no chances.

"Yes, sir!" the techs called, quickly setting about their duties.

We'd duck into nullspace and emerge on the other side of Xelthufed until the other ship's purpose in entering this particular system became clear.

I punched into the ship's computer. "War tact grid," I said.

Immediately it projected a three-dimensional map of the area around the *Falcon* onto my retina. The space was divided into a series of cubes. My ship was in the map's exact middle, the star-creatures were at one end and the Nemesis Class cruiser at the other. Various spots of yellow appeared on the Nemesis—the energy weapons.

Around the *Falcon*, various tube-shaped holes

appeared—the best routes into nullspace. I picked one. It would take us out-system for a few light-years, then around to the other side of Xelthufed. I didn't think any captain would think to follow us there.

"The other ship's weapons are powering up in preparation to fire," Jamis reported.

"Prepare for nullspace slip, window B-2," I said. "On my command. . . ."

"Wait!" Jamis said. "It's a Patrol ship. They're signalling their registration code . . . verified! It is a Patrol ship—the *Vortex Blaster.* Their captain is signalling. His name is Barlen Toff. He wishes to speak with you."

I leaned back. "Grant him permission. Drop the force shield as a sign of good will . . . but keep the Red Alert— and continue with preparation for the nullspace slip."

"Yes, sir."

So, the Patrol had arrived. Who tipped them as to our presence in this system, one of the spies Ulega Max claimed were on board? I'd find out soon enough. Glancing down at my clothes, I realized I needed to change into a dress uniform. If nothing else, the proper courtesy had to be shown to another captain when he came aboard. Barlen Toff . . . the name wasn't familiar.

The intercom crackled with static as Toff tried to open a channel to me. I decided to talk to him, but audio only. I punched the button.

"This is Captain Toff," he said.

"Captain Corrian here," I replied. "How may I serve the Patrol?"

"Deactivate your weapons and prepare to surrender all your data on this system."

"You're excedeing your authority."

"We have reports that this is military situation."

There must be a Patrol spy on board, I thought. How

else could they have found us—and our "military situation?" And why else would they have entered the system with their weapons charged and their shields raised? "There is no 'military situation.' Your reports are in error."

"We will be the judge of that."

I hesitated. As an instrument of the League's justice, the Patrol left a lot to be desired. Patrol captains this far from the center of galactic civilization tended to fall into two categories: some were pirates in all but name, often demanding bribes, working with smugglers and cut-throats, and generally putting personal gain ahead of duty. Others were militant glory-seekers, looking only for the battles that would win them fame and promotion—even if they had to create situations for the battles. The serious, well-meaning, honest Patrol captain was a relative rarity way out here.

If I turned my reports on the system over to Toff, and if he were looking for a battle, and if the star-creatures were hostile, there would certainly be a fight. And then the Patrol would shut down the system and might even cause Xelthufed to nova in order to get rid of the threat. Of course we could always find another red giant to skim . . . but the thought of destroying a sentient race was abhorrent to me.

It appeared that the aliens were friendly. They'd shown no sign of anger or hatred since their attack. And that attack might have been made out of fear. But if they *were* hostile? Biding their time to destroy us all?

"Captain Corrian," Toff said, "you must surrender the data to me now."

I decided to turn over the data. If the aliens were friendly, hopefully the Patrol wouldn't be able to goad them into a fight. If they were hostile, let the Patrol handle it. I'd done all I could. And I certainly wasn't about to cross this Patrol captain! *Turn to page 137.*

I'll keep the data and destroy it before I turn it over to the Patrol. Helping a sentient race survive is more important than anything else. *Turn to page 150.*

DEFIANCE!

I decided to ingore Ipijar's orders—after all, everything he'd ordered was blatantly against the *Falcon*'s interests. He'd probably been alerted by one of the spies on board!

I opened a channel to his ship. Though nobody answered my signal, I knew they'd be listening.

"Captain Ipijar, what you demand is unacceptable. Therefore, I will consider you and your ship as pirates—renegades, rather than officers of the Patrol and the League. Any attempt to approach my ship will be met with laser-fire. Corrian out."

Ordering the computer to put up the war tact grid, I kept a careful watch on the *S. P. Somtow* just in case Ipijar tried a sudden attack. I wouldn't have put it past him to try and seize my ship unexpectedly.

"Should I sound the alert, sir?" Jamis asked.

I nodded. "Yes. And scramble the shuttle crews to their ships—it looks like we're going to have a fight on our hands."

"Aye, sir." I heard him calling the First Guard and passing on my orders.

Ulega Max appeared on my command chair's monitor. He frowned, his face dark. "What do you think you're doing?" he demanded.

"Protecting the ship's interests," I said. "I don't have time to talk to you now. Make it quick."

"See that nothing happens to the starskimming equipment," he said. Then his image winked out.

Taking a deep breath, I let myself slip into the cool, emotionless fighting mindset the Academy had drilled into me. I took in outside information, evaluated it instantly, and filed it away for future use. I didn't let my feelings get in the way. In this state, I'd serve as a sort of human war computer.

Then I entered the war tact grid. The ship's computer projected a three-dimensional image on my retinas. Immediately a set of lines appeared, dividing the Aldema system, of which Xelthufed was a part, into a series of cubes. The star itself occupied the far right of the screen, while the *Falcon* and the *S. P. Somtow* hovered on the left. And Ipijar's ship was still closing with mine.

Hearing a soft beep at my right ear, I said, "Corrian here."

"Commander Omm, Captain. Three Blackmarks are ready to launch."

"The fourth is being held in reserve?"

"We shouldn't need it against a Scout."

"I know. Launch, then, and good luck."

"Thank you, sir."

As I watched the grid, the *Falcon's* docking bays opened and my shuttles slowly moved out. Their hundred-odd gun hatches drew back and laser-turrets appeared, along with atomic cannons and all the other sophisticated weapons and defense systems ships used in space. Thrusters flaring, the shuttles spread out and headed toward the *S. P. Somtow* at a steady rate.

"Raise the force shield," I said. Now that the shuttles were clear, I didn't have to worry about accidentally overloading their shields.

Ipijar's ship changed course abruptly, turning one side toward us. Its gun-turrets shot off one quick round— several dazzling balls of white light leaping toward the foremost shuttle. But it was just a warning shot, too weak to do damage. It diffused before hitting anything.

I gritted my teeth. Distantly, at my left ear, I could hear the intershuttle chatter as the computer descrambled it for me. Commander Omm ordered the others to spread apart and increase the power to their shields, and the various shuttle captains made their terse replies.

Then Captain Ipijar's voice came over the intercom. "Corrian, by the power of the League I order you to recall your shuttles. My reinforcements will be here soon—I'd hate to have to use them."

His voice must've been on all bands, for Commander Omm came on over the scrambled intershuttle channel a moment later. "Captain Corrian—do you want us to retreat?"

"Hold your positions, but don't attack," I told her. Then I opened communications with the *S. P. Somtow*. "Captain Ipijar?"

"What, Corrian?"

"Pull your ship back. I'm always willing to talk. But understand this—you're not taking my ship. To do so would violate League laws."

"Violate League laws? I don't know what you're talking about. Haven't you heard? The League's at war with the T'T'Ixions. Martial Law is in force . . . and that means you do what the Patrol says."

"The Patrol being you."

"Of course."

The T'T'Ixions? Who are they? I wondered. I'd never heard of them, and I knew myself to be familiar with most of the different races who ever fought the League. No, I'd certainly never heard of the T'T'Ixions—and then I guessed Ipijar was lying. It was just more evidence that he wasn't a Patrol captain.

I told him as much.

"Very well, Corrian. You've seen my ship's registration. I've identified myself as a Patrol Captian. You've been warned three times. Now you've sealed your fate." Static

---

119

crackled as he broke the connection.

I watched and waited, but he made no more attempts to communicate or attack. The Blackmark-model shuttles took up positions between his ship and mine, blocking his passage. I knew he had at least one more trick up his sleeve . . . but what?

I didn't feel like running from him. I figured I could stand him off, at least for a couple more days. Few pirates would wait around in a free system. He'd break and run as soon as he saw I wouldn't roll over and play dead.

The next few hours passed all too slowly. I'd begun to think his words were all bluff, that I could down-grade the alert, when I saw Jamis jump. Before he could call a warning, I ducked back into the war tact grid. He'd seen something on his monitors, and it had startled or frightened him—what?

Then, as I watched the space around the *S. P. Somtow,* the field of stars began to ripple and blur . . . the grid lines wavered . . . and something began to emerge from null space. . . .

I gasped in shock as three Planet-Busters—the largest, most powerful ships ever built in known space—suddenly materialized to flank the *S. P. Somtow.* These were huge ring-shaped craft, each measuring three or four kilometers in diameter, each slowly spinning around a half-kilometer-wide silver-colored sphere. That sphere channeled a devastating beam of energy, enough power to blast a whole planet apart. Enough power even to nova a sun! It was frightening to think of what such a blast would do to the *Falcon* and her crew!

And the Blackmark-model shuttles—they were like tiny corks afloat in one of those legendary terrestrial seas, lost among the waves. Such small ships would be swept aside like dust during the Planet-Busters' attack.

I screened out the frantic calls from the shuttle commanders, ignored Jamis's frantic request for instructions. Captain Ipijar was calling me. I punched the intercom button and his gloating face appeared.

"Well, Captain Corrian, now that my friends have arrived, are you prepared to surrender your ship?"

"Yes," I said shortly. I had a sinking feeling inside, but I was damned if he'd see me sweat.

"Good. I'm sending my shuttle over now. You are to consider yourself under arrest until your trial—"

My sinking feeling got worse, but I gritted my teeth.

"—for breaking martial laws. You were warned, Corrian, as the records will clearly show."

"Very well. Send your shuttle over. I will recall my Blackmarks. You will meet no resistance—the crew will cooperate with the League and the Patrol."

"Do so." And then his image winked out.

I leaned back and let the harsh reality sink in. I'd made a terrible mistake in choosing to defy Ipijar. I knew that now . . . but 20/20 hindsight didn't help. A numbness came over me, and I couldn't concentrate on anything for a long minute.

"Sir, your orders?" Jamis said, bringing me back to reality.

"Recall Commander Omm and the others. And . . . that's it. My last order, as captain of this ship."

"Sir!" Jamis's face was white.

I shook my head, sincerely touched at his obvious distress. But already I could see Captain Ipijar's shuttle leaving the *S. P. Somtow's* rear docking bay—I didn't have much time. "I'll speak to the Ship's Council," I said. "Let the crew know what happened. Assure them that they won't be held responsible for my actions."

"Aye, sir." Jamis swallowed, then turned back to his

console and I could hear him speaking over the in-ship intercom. His tones were hushed, as though at a funeral.

And, I thought, it probably would be a funeral—mine. Not in the literal sense, of course—the Patrol might be harsh, but they didn't kill prisoners. I'd pretty well killed my career, though, by coming up against the Patrol and losing. Who would hire me now, after the Ship's Council threw me off the *Falcon*, or after the Patrol sent me to one of its prison planets?

Slowly, reluctantly, I went to see the Ship's Council. From the speed of the *S. P. Somtow's* shuttle, I guessed I still had fifteen minutes before Ipijar's men arrived. I better savor my freedom as long as I could.

"Kel, Kel." Vimister Groll shook his head slowly. I felt a growing sense of shame and helplessness. "I'm quite disappointed—I held high expectations for you." He sighed.

"What's done is done," Ulega Max said sternly. He paced the room like a caged animal, as though *he* were about to be arrested, rather than me. "We will, of course, try and get you freed, Kel. But don't hold your breath. You're not of Trader blood, and what influence we can bring to bear will be very limited."

"I understand that." I stared at the floor, resigned to my fate. It had become obvious that the Ship's Council didn't have enough powerful friends—or wasn't willing to call in enough old debts—to get me freed.

Groll sighed again. "Alack and alas—the time has come for all good men . . . and for you, too, Kel Corrian. Captain Ipijar's shuttle will be here in moments—and you must meet it."

"Of course. And—thank you for all you've done, and all you'll do to get me out of this mess." Bowing in ritual

Free Trader fashion, I backed from the room. The door slid open and I found myself in the hallway.

There was a loud buzzing in my ears and I could feel my heart beating heavily in my chest. I'd felt this way only once before . . . when, as a child, I'd gone into the Headmaster's office to report a grave infraction of the Academy's rules—and to name myself as chief culprit. But I'd done worse than break curfew and go exploring Deneb Station in the dark this time, and I knew my punishment would be worse than the Academy's slap on the wrist for first offenders. I tried to swallow and found I couldn't get past the lump in my throat.

I headed for my quarters to change into my dress uniform. At least, I could go in style.

In military cases, a panel of Patrol captains becomes judge, jury, and executioner. Like now.

I stood before three gray-uniformed old men, in a small, gray room, aboard the *Bloody Mary*—one of the Planet-Busters. The men were all Admirals in the Patrol, and I'd never seen a more dour lot. Their faces held not a trace of sympathy or understanding for my case.

They read the charges once. "Kel Corrian, Captain on the Trader ship *Marrow Falcon*, you failed to obey the orders of the Patrol during a military situation. You threatened a Patrol ship. You threatened a Patrol captain."

I had no chance to agree or disagree. The charges were statements. The record spoke for itself.

The Admiral on the right spoke next. His wispy gray hair and round, white face made him the most congenial-looking one of the three, but his eyes remained dark and hard.

"Corrian, we've been over the transcript and tapes a half-dozen times. We can understand your paranoia about strange ships, considering your age and status—and the dangerous times in which we live. And we also realize the report Captain Ipijar had received about you was in error—our men have been over the *Marrow Falcon* thoroughly and can find no evidence of smuggling drugs, or of any other crime. Therefore our sentence is as lenient as it can be."

I straightened. Now would come my fate.

"You are sentenced to labor on Duane's World, for three months."

The words were like a savage blow. I felt my heart beating in my throat. My chest constricted. The salt mines of Duane's World were notorious as a harsh punishment! People died there all the time—from the heat, the dust, the back-breaking physical labor. It was a place they sent people to die.

I was so shaken I almost missed their next words.

"The sentence is suspended. Your record is clear of previous infractions, so you will be allowed to continue with your work—this time. You will spend three more days aboard this ship while the final details are taken care of."

"Thank you, sirs—" I began, shaking in sudden relief. But they'd turned away and begun to file out through the back door.

A black-uniformed Patrol guard was pulling my right arm. "Come on," he said.

I followed him willingly, to find Vimister Groll and the other two Ship's Council members waiting outside.

"May I talk to them for a moment?" I asked the guard.

He hesitated, then nodded. "Yes. But it can't take long. You're due in processing in fifteen minutes."

"What did they decide?" Groll demanded.

"I've been sentenced to labor in the mines on Duane's World, but—"

"The mines," Groll said softly. There was a stunned look on his face.

"But," I said, "the sentence has been suspended. I'll spend a few days here, then be free to go."

Vimister Groll leaned forward, chuckling. "Ah, boy, listen well—when you're released, the *Falcon* will be yours again."

I just looked at him, startled, hardly able to believe what he'd said. "Then you'll wait for me?"

"Of course," Ulega Max growled. "You risked your life to protect the ship several times. That loyalty is rare among those who aren't of Trader blood. We'd be crazy to let you escape."

I didn't know what to say. A warm, satisfied feeling began to build inside me. They'd wait for me—the *Falcon* would still be my ship!

The guard pulled on my arm, and as we headed down the long, dark corridor, I shouted over my shoulder, "Thank you, sirs, for everything!"

THE END

JEWELS FOR IPIJAR

I would surrender peacefully to the Patrol. After all, I'd done nothing illegal. This whole mess was probably some bureaucratic mistake. It was my duty as a citizen of the League to accede to the Patrol's will. To even think of fighting them—no matter what the reason—could only end in disaster.

The static cleared and I looked at Ipijar's face again. "Well?" he demanded.

"Of course you're welcome to come aboard, Captain Ipijar. We have nothing to hide from the Patrol. We seek only to stay within the League's laws—as you must know, from our records."

He leaned forward, staring into the monitor. "Oh, I know all about the *Falcon*'s records, make no mistake. Suspected of smuggling, drug-running, supplying black market goods on a dozen worlds. . . ."

"Speak of facts, not suspicions, Captain."

He smiled coldly, like a Centauran bluesnake about to strike. "Of course. Since you're so willing to cooperate, I won't bring my men aboard to assume control. The Patrol always takes loyalty into consideration in its decisions, as you must know. Therefore you may keep command of your ship, Corrian—for now. I'll take a shuttle over with several of my techs. We want to check over some of your equipment. You have no objections, of course." It was a statement.

I nodded. "No objections—at the moment."

He frowned. "Very well, then." And his image winked out.

Jamis said, "One of the *S. P. Somtow's* rear shuttle bays is opening."

"They won't waste any time in getting here. I guess I'd better meet them. Keep me informed if anything unexpected happens."

"Aye, sir," he said.

Twenty minutes later, I met Captain Ipijar at the *Falcon*'s main docking bay, and my initial impressions grew stronger. Captain Ipijar was a short man, small boned, with gray skin and grayer eyes. He was still sneering, and looked like he never stopped—as though the expression were frozen onto his face.

Swaggering over to me, he said bluntly, "Hurry up, Corrian, I've got better things to do than let you waste my time. Where's that special drug-manufacturing equipment you've got on board?"

"I'm sorry, but—"

"Snap to it! I know all about it. Reports were transmitted to the Patrol base on Darrelless VI giving full details. Now I want to see the equipment that processes superheated gas into hallucinogenic drugs—or I'll have my men tear apart your ship until they find it."

"You're making a mistake. We're processing the gas into jewels, not drugs."

That caught him off-guard a moment. But a moment only. "Show me."

"As you wish, Captain Ipijar, you may look at the equipment for starskimming, but your techs can't. The process is classified Ship's Business."

"It's also illegal."

"Not at all."

He hesitated, obviously considering the problems of trying to circumvent classified Ship's Business. There would be a lot of red-tape involved: special waivers from Patrol Headquarters, appeals from the Ship's Council . . . it could drag on for month after month. From his expression, I could tell he didn't like the idea. I relaxed. He'd have to go strictly by the League's laws, at least wherever it might show up on official transcripts. At last he nodded.

"All right, no techs. But I will inspect the machinery myself."

I smiled. "Fine." *And your men won't be able to discover the actual processing method, Captain, and you won't be able to copy it for your own private gain,* I added mentally.

Then I turned toward the nearest lift, saying to Ipijar, "Please follow me, sir."

"That's better." He motioned for the three Patrol techs behind him to wait, then fell into step behind me, almost—but not quite—walking on my heels. I walked faster and got farther ahead of him.

Entering the lift, we headed down to the sixth level, then walked through the hall and over to the processing room's door. With typical aloofness, Ipijar pushed past me and shoved the door open, startling the two white-coated techs on duty within. I remembered their names, a bit to my surprise: Tech Glassglow, with his blue eyes and white-blond hair, and Tech Wuthoqquan, who was fatter, with dark skin, a bald head, and a piercing black eyes. Both men wore heavy gold double-helix pendants around their necks.

"Sir?" Glassglow called to me.

I motioned reassuringly to him. "Relax—it's not a surprise inspection. The Patrol just wants to take a quick look at our equipment."

"But—" he started.

I glared at him and he shut up, taking my meaning at once—*Don't let the Patrol know anything more than you have to!*

Not much of the processing equipment could be seen in the laboratory—just the huge metal box that occupied the center of the room. Ipijar walked around it, looking at the pipes running into it from the ceiling, examining the conveyor belt. The machine stood eight meters high, another eight wide, and five deep. Various dials and digital readouts covered most of its visible surface. Small lights blinked at regular intervals. It hummed softly, like a hive of bees.

Captain Ipijar walked around it once, frowning. His training in the Patrol wouldn't have given him much of a technical background, outside of the standard courses in weapons maintenance, hull repair, nullspace theory, and all the other courses all cadets had to take—that's why I'd let him see the equipment.

He tapped the box with the toe of his right boot (the techs wincing visibly as he did), grunted once, then said, "I want to see it work."

I stared at him, astounded. "That's classified Ship's Business. I've told you what it does." All I could think of was creating more of those sentient jewels.

Ipijar snorted. "So you did, so you did. But I've been a Patrol captain for a long, long time, and I didn't reach my rank by believing everything I hear about a Trader ship, even what the ship's captain tells me."

"I refuse to allow this—"

He cut me off with a sudden slash of his hand. "No, Corrian. You have no say in the matter. If you try and stop me, I'll have you arrested for hindering a Patrol investigation."

"There are laws—"

"Only the Patrol's, now, with Martial Law in effect." He pronounced the final words with biting enthusiasm.

"What?" I demanded. "Martial Law? What're you

talking about?"

"Oh? Haven't you heard? The League's at war with the T'T'Ixians. They've invaded five member-worlds already."

I frowned skeptically. "I haven't heard anything—"

He shrugged. "Oh, it's on the other side of the known universe, not here. I have little chance of actually taking part in a battle. But Martial Law is extended through the League, even to this barren system, and I'm not going to forget it."

Or let me forget it, I thought. I said nothing. There was nothing I could do to stop him and he knew it.

Ipijar motioned to the techs. "Go on, start the machine. I want to see for myself exactly what it does. Jewels or drugs—we'll soon get to the bottom of this!"

"It's dangerous," I said. "I won't allow the processing to start!"

"Then how can I see that it doesn't process drugs?"

"You'll just have to trust me, Captain."

"Start it."

Techs Glassglow and Wuthoqquan looked at me. "Sir?" Glassglow said, hesitantly. "There's still some gas left in the holding tank. Should we?"

Captain Ipijar raged at them. "Do it now, or I'll have you arrested!"

They turned pale, and I hesitated. With Martial Law in effect, he had the power to do so and, somehow, I had the feeling he'd follow through on his threat. Reluctantly, I turned to the techs. "Go ahead," I told them. Then I turned to Ipijar, shrugging helplessly. "But this is against my protests—I want that known."

"I'll make a note of it."

"And I want to give you a warning: the jewels we made were sentient. They tried to take over the minds of my

---

130

crew. That's why I stopped the manufacturing process in this system. If you force us to make more jewels, it could lead to trouble."

He stared at me a moment, then gave his approximation of a grin. It looked like a smile on a corpse. "And you expect me to believe that story?"

"It's the truth."

"Jewels taking over men's minds—it's crazy! Not even a madman would believe that." He turned to the Wuthoqquan and Glassglow. "Carry on."

The two techs scurried to their positions, shock and fear apparent on their faces. They called numbers to one another as they went over the controls carefully, setting up for the manufacturing process.

I backed over to the shelf holding Luathek's sound box, then picked the machine up. I'd had several of them made and distributed to key parts of the ship, in case of more trouble. If the jewels we produced now started to take control of my men, I'd be ready to shatter their internal structure with sound-waves.

Ipijar was too preoccupied with the techs to notice what I was doing. I slipped the box into my pocket, carefully keeping my finger near the button.

"Hurry up, there!" Ipijar growled.

"Yes, sir!" Wuthoqquan called. "We're ready to start now, sir." Crossing over to a small Off/On switch on the far wall, he paused there, looking around the room. I could see him making one final mental check of the equipment. Beside me, Ipijar shifted impatiently.

"Hurry up," he said again.

"Ready here," Glassglow reported, gulping slightly.

Tech Wuthoqquan pulled the switch.

For an instant, nothing happened. Then I heard a low noise far in the distance, a throbbing chump-chump-

chump sound. The humming grew louder and louder, building steadily toward a screaming crescendo. Overhead, the light panels flickered. I saw the two techs, their terrified faces looked like masks.

Sweat rolled down my face. The room had suddenly grown stiflingly hot, as though a furnace door had opened and a hot wind blasted over me. Water condensed on the sides of the equipment and ran down to the floor, where it vanished down small drains.

Still the hum grew louder. The conveyor belt began to move. Out rolled eight beautiful cut jewels, each glowing white-hot.

"We must wait for them to cool now, sir," Wuthoqquan said. "It won't take long."

Ipijar's eyes were wide, his jaw went slack. He stared at the jewels with a kind of puzzled amazement.

I kept my hand close to my pocket, close to the button, just in case anything happened. I wouldn't hesitate to destroy the crystals if they seemed at all dangerous.

At last the computer beeped, signalling that the jewels were ready. Glassglow stepped forward and picked up two egg-sized gems. They shone with a white luminescence unlike anything found on a planet, in each facet hung a miniature star. The tech started to walk over to Ipijar, but the captain leaped forward, grabbing both jewels from Glassgow's hand. Ipijar held them almost reverently in his hands, gazing deep into their glowing hearts. And, like a man in love, I saw his features soften, a smile tugged at the corners of his mouth. He sighed softly.

Then he looked up at me, and his face grew hard and cruel once more. There was a calculating look in his eyes, as if he'd begun to realize how much such gems would be worth on the open market . . . easily more money than he'd make in a lifetime.

I looked at the jewels he still held. They seemed harmless enough now. If Ipijar was possessed, it was only by his own greed. I wondered when—if ever—they'd come to life and start taking over the minds of people around them. How had it happened to us the first time? Nobody seemed sure.

And a horrifying thought occurred to me: If these two jewels—or whatever sentience lurked within them—had been in contact with the other crystals during the take-over . . . maybe they'd learned enough about our race to know how to wait, how to bide their time until our defenses were down and they could strike without fear of being caught or destroyed?

"Captain," Ipijar growled as he turned to the door. "Come with me. I want to speak with you privately."

I followed him out into the corridor, then stopped when the processing room's door shut behind us. "How about here?"

He glanced meaningfully at the video monitor at the end of the hall. "I said privately."

I didn't like the sound of that. "Let me guess," I said. "You have a proposition I can't refuse."

He only smiled. His lips twisted cruelly, and I knew I wouldn't like what I heard.

I took him to one of the private conference rooms. It was a small chamber decorated all in shades of blue, with pale walls, a soft carpet of azure, and a sky-blue ceiling with a checkerboard pattern of light-panels and repellers. A table had been bolted to the middle of the floor, and a scattering of formchairs surrounded it. It was a comfortable, relaxing, completely private place.

He stood in the doorway, glanced around once, then nodded. "This will do. There are no monitors here?"

"Would I lie to you?" I asked.

Not deigning to answer, he strutted in and flopped down in the nearest chair. It molded itself to his body. Setting one jewel on the table, he held the other up to his right eye, gazing deep into its white depths.

"Beautiful," he said.

"Valuable," I said. Taking a seat on the opposite side of the table, I studied him. He seemed completely absorbed in the jewel. "What did you want to tell me?"

He set the gem on the table, beside the first. "Only that I've decided you're perfectly within your legal rights to mine this star. As far as I can see, that machine of yours couldn't make drugs."

"And?"

"Well, you know how bureaucracies like the Patrol work, how many months can be spent just filing the papers to get your ship cleared from Patrol custody. We go to a lot of trouble to help Free Trader ships, to keep the spaceways safe and clear of pirates. It's a lot of hard work . . . with notoriously low pay."

"I think I know where you're heading," I said. "You want these two jewels. A bribe."

He smiled. His eyes glittered with greed. "No, not a bribe at all. Think of it as advance pay for services rendered. I'll clear your ship within the week—push all the papers through as quickly as I can—and then you'll be free to leave. Nobody'll ever know about the jewels. After all, these two baubles aren't on your list of gems you've manufactured, now are they?"

"And if I say no?"

"Then you'll rot here for the next eight or nine months. I have a messy desk. Things can get lost on it very easily."

I swallowed, thinking of the profits we'd lose if we stayed here very long. It might be enough to put the ship in debt . . . and the Ship's Council certainly wouldn't like that.

Would two jewels matter that much? Who would miss them?

But what about the risks? What if they did come to life and take over Ipijar and his men—what then? What if the jewels tried to use him against his crew and the Patrol? No, I certainly couldn't risk that. . . .

Ipijar had already pocketed the gems. He stood, as though he considered our deal already concluded.

"I'll leave now," he said. "You, doubtless, have much to do to get your ship in order."

Then I made my decision. "The gems are yours—on one condition."

"What's that?"

"You listen to a warning about them."

He laughed. "Another warning about how the crystals are going to come to life and attack me? You're little game's over, Captain. You lost. Give it up."

"There really is a sentience in the crystals. It has the ability to take over men's minds—it almost took over most of my crew. Luckily, we came up with a defense against them." I took the sound-box from my pocket and set it on the table before him.

"What's that?" Ipijar demanded, sniggering.

"It's a weapon I want you to take. It generates sound-waves that shatter the crystals' inner structure. It also kills whatever's inside them."

"That would ruin them!"

"Yes . . . but would you rather have a flawed jewel or be possessed by an alien?"

"You're crazy!" He sneered. "Or lying. I don't believe you—you're just trying to keep me from taking them!"

"No, I'm not. I—"

"Shut up, Corrian. If you say one more word, the deal's off . . . and I'll keep these baubles anyway. I tried to be nice. I tried to give you something for them. Don't make me regret it."

Biting my lip, I grew silent. *I'd* tried to be nice too. I'd tried to warn him. I'd even offered him the sound-box. What more could I do?

In a brooding, angry silence, we both walked back to the docking bay. Ipijar's three techs still waited there, and after he waved them back into his shuttle, he turned to me once more.

"I'll forget what happened in the conference room, Corrian, for your sake," he snarled. "I'm not a man without conscience."

"Thanks," I said, "sir." I couldn't keep a trace of bitterness from my voice.

He laughed. Then he turned and strode through the airlock, and that was the last I ever saw of him.

We were allowed to leave the system within the week, just as he'd promised. At least he kept his word. And we never had another problem with the Patrol.

Once, just out of curiosity, I went back to the Patrol Base at Deneb Station and tried to trace Captain Ipijar's career—to see if he'd managed to keep the jewels from taking control of him and his crew. In his record I found only a small notation.

Ipijar, Felwoon; captain of the Patrol Scout S. P. Somtow, which disappeared during a routine patrol of the Aldema Proxima system. Assumed dead. (See also Scout S. P. Somtow for a full list of crewmen aboard.)

THE END

THE S'CHASS

I decided to give Toff the data. After all, the star-creatures did not seem overtly hostile. They'd had a chance to destroy the *Marrow Falcon* when her shields and computers were down, but hadn't done so—which proved they meant us no harm. And yet, I wondered if Captain Toff would see it that way. . . .

"Captain Corrian," he said again, a note of impatience creeping into his voice, "I want that data now, not next year. I don't have time to play games with you. Under League law, you must turn the information over to me—or face the consequences."

I touched the intercom button. "Very well, Captain. We will now begin transmitting." Motioning to Jamis to start the transfer of data, I sat back and folded my arms to wait. Barlen Toff would call me again—as soon as he'd made a preliminary analysis of what we'd given him, as soon as he realized we'd made contact with an alien race.

Sure enough, after fifteen minutes, the communication light flashed suddenly. I jabbed the button. "What now, Captain Toff?" I said.

"You," he said, "are ordered to place your ship temporarily under my command during the duration of this emergency. New directives will follow."

"What emergency?" I demanded. "None exists. You're exceeding your authority, Captain!"

"Not at all. Your ship was attacked by intelligent beings who don't belong to the League. That makes Xelthufed a combat zone. Until I find out just who these aliens are, and what their intentions may be, the possibility of more fighting still exists. I may need your weapons—your Blackmark-model shuttles especially—before the day is through. If you have any complaints, please contact the nearest League Judicial Station." I could almost hear him laughing as he added, "That's Arcturus—only forty-one short light-years away."

And, I knew, a message would take nine days to get there and back, even through nullspace. I cursed bitterly, feeling completely helpless. The Patrol manipulated League laws and justice to their own designs. I never should have turned the data over to Toff, I realized—I should've destroyed it first and attributed the destruction to a computer error. It would've made my life immeasurably simpler.

"We were not attacked," I said, trying to keep my voice calm and steady, though I knew it wouldn't do any good. Patrol captains see everything in a military light.

"You were. Any unauthorized entry, damage to equipment, and theft of information is an attack. I don't have time to argue with you. Either agree to my terms or I'll have you relieved of duty. Several of my lieutenants would like nothing more than a temporary command. . . ."

"Very well," I told him bitterly. "We will await your instructions." I waited long enough to make it an insult. "Sir."

"According to the information you sent me, your men have assembled a communication device. Is this correct?"

"Yes. Sir."

"My men will cross over to your ship and take control of it. They will, of course, work aboard the *Marrow Falcon*—with the voluntary aid of your techs—until such time as I see fit to release the equipment."

"Is that an order or a request?"

"See that they receive your full cooperation." He ignored my question, switched off his intercom and left me listening to static.

Nothing remained for me to do but bide my time . . . watch the aliens . . . and try to find Barlen Toff's spy.

I was on my way to my cabin to change into a dress uniform when Ulega Max appeared from the lift ahead. Four guards flanked him. He strode up to me, cape swirling, and stopped in my path

"What is it?" I said, trying to keep my patience.

"You gave in to him too easily! Now everything will be ruined!"

"What did you want me to do? Fight him?"

"If necessary, yes!"

I sighed. "Look, Ulega, don't think the idea didn't occur to me. We could've run. I almost nullspaced to the other side of the sun to gain more time, but I didn't. I think the star-creatures are friendly. Think of the possible benefits if they are—and if we're the first to open up trade relations with them!"

"What could they possibly want of ours?"

"Technology. And we want to skim their sun . . . in the safest way possible. With them as supervisors. . . ?"

The idea seemed to appeal to him, for he stepped back with a slight nod. "You seem to have the situation under control." He sounded surprised.

"That's what you're paying me for. Now," I said, "dismiss your guards and come into my cabin for a drink. There are several matters of a more . . . delicate nature that I must discuss with you."

"Very well." He motioned for the guards to wait for him, then followed me to my cabin. After I touched the handpad and the door dilated, we both entered.

We sat in the antechamber to my bedroom, at a small table, and sipped Jurisnac brandy from small nippled spheres. Neither of us said anything for a few moments.

"Now," I said, "I have a serious complaint to make."

"What is it?" Ulega asked. The brandy had calmed him, and he smiled at me almost patronizingly, in a detached sort of way. I realized, then, that he saw me as just one more creature of his, someone easily manipulated and ordered about.

I said, as tactfully as I could, "That wasn't the first time you've confronted me in front of crewmen. If you have complaints about my performance of duty, then you're to speak to me in private. I can not have my authority undermined. I know you, as a leader yourself, will appreciate the point I make."

"Yes . . . yes, perhaps you're right. But still, when you do such things and they seem detrimental to the good of the ship—"

"You never gave me a chance to file a report with the Ship's Council," I pointed out. "All would've been explained there. I can understand your need to eavesdrop on private communications—after all, your only concern is the *Falcon*—but you must let me do my job. Or I'll be forced to take matters into my own hands."

He stared at me a moment, trying—I think—to decide whether he was furious or pleased at my courage. Finally, he stood a bit unsteadily, smiled at me, said, "As you say, Captain," then turned and wandered toward the door. It dilated for him. He was gone and I was alone.

One more difficulty solved, I thought. Only . . . why did it seem that with every solution came ten more problems?

I went to meet the delegation from the *Vortex Blaster* in the third docking tube an hour later. I'd changed into my best uniform—a deep red silk shirt, black pants and boots, a gold sash around my waist to mark my rank as captain. I'd managed to put most of my anger and frustration aside, and it was with a genuine measure of welcome that I greeted Captain Toff's people when they stepped from the airlock.

There were six of them—four women, one man, and a small, round, gray-furred Calgiri of indeterminate sex. They carried, between them, several cases of equipment mounted on null-grav sleds.

The Calgiri came up to me and saluted with one of his four triple-jointed arms. He wore a translator-box around his neck, from which a thin, whistly voice emerged. "Captain Corrian?"

I nodded. "Yes. You are?"

A series of clicks and whistles. "You may to address me as 'Wing'—it is a friend-name to give to me by humans." And then he told me the names of the others in the group. "We will to study the machine and to work to contact the star-creatures. Our task must to start at once."

"As you say, Wing. I've ordered cabins prepared for you and the others."

"They are to lie near the communication equipment?"

"On the same level, yes. First Tech Luathek will show you the way. If you have any problems with the arrangements, please contact me and I will see what can be done."

I turned to the Pavian as Wing murmured, "To be most acceptable."

"Yes, Kel?" Luathek said.

"Please take care of our guests. See to it they have everything they need."

"Yes, Kel. That I will accomplish." Turning, he gestured to the Calgiri. "This way, please, Citizen."

I spent the next two days on the bridge, skimming through the League's laws governing the Patrol. As far as I could see, Toff hadn't actually done anything outside the legal scope of his power. I couldn't get him off my back on some technicality.

As I worked, the Ship's Council periodically sent me little notes through the computer. Since they all bore Priority One clearance through the information net, they blanked out the data on my screen, repeating the same essential message (though in politer terms) over and over again: "You're the captain, so get us out of this mess. We're losing all our profits here."

I trashed the notes and continued with my research, to no avail.

On the third day I got a frantic message from Luathek. I pushed the vid button. Gesturing wildly, he shouted, "Kel! They are stealing all the work of mine! You must get about ordering them to leave it here!"

"Calm down," I said. "What do you mean? What're they stealing?"

"The communication device for talking with the starcreatures! Kel, they're pulling it through the door on a null-grav sled. Stop them!"

"Wait there," I said. "I'll join you in a second." Rising, I headed toward the door.

By the time I reached the laboratory area, Jol Mellawithe and Luathek were engaged in a loud argument with Wing and two of Captain Toff's other people. The other three blue-uniformed crewmen waited off to the side, the machine Luathek had built held between them. I could see the shimmer of low-power repeller fields around the sled's base.

They'd been trying to smuggle it off the ship . . . and I could only conclude that Captain Toff had put them up to it. They must've discovered something—something that made Toff want complete control of communications with the creatures. What?

"What's the meaning of this?" I demanded.

Wing looked at me in silence for a second. "It has been to me ordered for the equipment to be on the *Vortex Blaster.*"

"They can't do that, can they, Captain?" Jol Mellawithe cried. "Just when we were making progress!"

"Progress?" I asked, startled.

"Yes, sir! We were starting to get intelligible questions from the creatures when these vacuum-heads began unplugging everything and ordering Luathek and me into the next room!"

"Captain Toff ordered this?" I asked Wing.

"Yes. I must to install it on the *Vortex Blaster.*"

I hesitated. The theft was well within Toff's legal rights as a Patrol captain. I'd read about 'Seizure of Vital Goods' in the League laws. Toff would've known I'd know. And I knew he'd know I knew. . . .

I couldn't do anything but give in. Shrugging helplessly, I said to Wing, "Take it away, but I want a receipt—and make sure you don't damage anything. I'll want it back when you're done with it."

"Captain!" Jol cried in dismay.

"Kel!" Luathek echoed him.

I shook my head.

"Yes, Captain Corrian," Wing whistled cheerfully. "Please to instruct your subordinates to move themselves, lest we to damage them inadvertently."

"They'll move out of your way," I said. "Won't you, Luathek? Jol?"

Grumbling, they stepped back and allowed Wing and the others to pass.

"Why did you do this?" Luathek said softly.

"They would've taken it by force otherwise. I'm going to see Captain Toff now—and hopefully everything will be straightened out."

"Yes, Kel," Luathek said. His voice held something I'd never heard from him before—bitterness, and more than a trace of disappointment. I knew I'd let him down, and it hurt. For that Captain Barlen Toff would have to pay!

I stalked into Barlen Toff's office. His aide—a dour-faced old man in a standard blue-and-gold uniform—looked up at me from a small, orderly desk in the far corner.

"Can I help you?"

"Yes," I said. "I'm Captain Corrian. I want to see Captain Toff. Now."

"Just a minute, sir," he said. He murmured something toward his desk, listened, then straightened and looked at me. "Captain Toff will be available in five minutes. If you would wait. . . ?"

"Very well," I snapped. "I'll wait!"

I paced up and down, trying to wear holes in the deck-plates, and with every turn I became more and more angry. What right did Toff have to seize Free Trader equipment? What right did he have to order my crew about as though he were the *Falcon*'s captain rather than me? Legally—yes, he could do it. But ethically? And there I hoped to catch him.

At last the aide said, "Captain Toff will see you now."

Like an emperor granting an audience to some peasant, I thought. I said nothing to the aide, but walked over to the door. It slid aside with a low hiss of air. I stepped through, and it shut almost on my heels.

The air inside wasn't Earth-normal; it held traces of sulfur and ozone and other things I couldn't quite identify—and the lighting was a murky yellow, almost as if Toff's eyes weren't used to the same sorts of suns as I was. Perhaps he came from a planet circling a yellow dwarf star.

He sat behind a large, disorganized-looking desk. Vid-tapes, datachips, and various papers were spread before him in a random pattern. And when he looked up at me, I realized I'd underestimated him by assuming he was the usual sort of Patrol militant.

He was slightly balding, with a wide face and large, dark, intelligent eyes. His dark blue uniform with gold trim was immaculate—a striking contrast to his work-area—and across his chest gleamed gold insignia from a dozen-odd battle campaigns. I recognized a few of them: Mongo-Mongo, where the Patrol had fought a pirate stronghold and suffered high casualties; Zontilux, where they'd beaten back the invading Bell Hordes; Dante and Spooch and Abernathy. The Patrol captains who'd been most eager to fight had rushed in first—and had died first. The most cautious and thoughtful had taken their time in picking targets. Even so, a lot of them had died, too.

That Captain Toff was a veteran of so many campaigns spoke well not only of his military record, but his ability to think under pressure . . . and his luck as a commander. I realized, then, that he'd already proved my initial assessments of him unfounded.

"Good day, Captain Corrian," he said. His voice was low and strong. He didn't rise or offer me his hand—but then, I hadn't expected him to.

Feeling my righteous indignation start to ooze out of me, I tried hard to latch onto my former anger. "Sir, I've come to talk to you about your decision to seize certain equipment from my ship."

"Before you get upset about that, I have one more order for you."

"What's that, sir?" I asked warily.

"Your ship's just been quarantined. You can't leave this

system without Patrol okay."

"What!"

He shrugged. "Not my idea, I assure you. I'd just as soon have you out-system. Prefer it, in fact."

"Why—"

He shrugged. "Incompetent bureaucratic red-tape, of course. Can't avoid it, not even out here."

I didn't know what to say.

"Talk," he said, "or get out. You're wasting my time."

Frustrated, I sputtered, "I protest this action, sir. You're cutting into my ship's profits. I demand you allow us to leave at once."

"No," he said. "Is that all?"

I was floundering. "You've stolen equipment from my ship. I want it back."

"You mean the communication equipment—"

"Your men can build their own, easily enough."

He nodded. "Yes, they could—but, again, it's a matter of secrecy. I don't want anyone but the Patrol to have the ability to communicate with the S'chass—the star-creatures, as you call them. This is a political move more than anything else, and you'll just have to trust me that it's for the best."

"Dismantle it before you return it, then!"

"I'm sorry, but no." He smiled. "You'd only put it back together again."

Then something he'd said brought me up short. "You called them the—what? S'chass?"

"Yes. We've just made full contact with them today. They were trying to warn you earlier to leave—that's why they went through the trouble of raiding your computer's data-banks and trying to learn Basic. It seems they're tele-pathically imprintable, or some such. They operate on emotions. They're perfectly peaceful so long as you're peaceful with them. But make a military move and . . . instant war. They're a potentially dangerous race to be around."

For the second time I didn't know what to say.

"You're young, Captain. I know your Ship's Council must be pressuring you. I give you this advice: tell them that, no matter what happens, they're entitled to the League's First Contact award. It's small—a hundred thousand royals—but that will more than pay for the equipment I've taken. And the Patrol will, of course, compensate you for lost funds . . . a million royals or so ought to cover it."

I gasped. "A million? But that's—"

"The least you're entitled to, considering the fortune you're not making by remaining here. I have full details on your starskimming operation from my operative on your ship. And yes, you can keep making those jewels; it's not the Patrol's business, and I have no interest in shutting down your ship, or robbing you."

"That's m-most kind, sir," I stammered.

"I've also changed my ruling on the system. You were right—Xelthufed isn't a combat zone, and it's going to stay that way. Nothing remains for you to do but wait. Be patient, and tell your Council the same."

"I guess that's all I can do, isn't it, sir?" I said, smiling weakly.

His smile broadened. "Yes, Captain."

I went back to the *Marrow Falcon*, brooding on all Toff'd said. A million royals . . . more than most Free Trader ships net in a year.

Meeting with the Ship's Council in their curious black room, I told them everything.

"And," I said, "Toff even conceded that we need a sizable award for lost profits."

"How much?" Ulega Max demanded.

"Around a million. Plus the award for making contact with the S'chass—the star-creatures. That's another hundred thousand royals."

Vimister Groll studied me shrewdly. "You're not of our people," he said, "but you have the right spirit. I've decided I like you, Kel Corrian. And I think you're going to be captain of the *Marrow Falcon* for a long, long time, if you've the desire to stay."

"Well," I said, hesitantly.

"I know we've been a bit rough on you—but times are hard. You've more than proven your worth."

"Thank you, sir," I said. "I think I'd like to stay here and work."

"Only one thing remains," Ulega snapped. "Get that damn quarantine lifted from the ship so we can be off!"

I smiled. "That shouldn't be a problem. We'll be out of this system before the week's through."

"We're declaring Xelthufed a Class V system," Captain Toff told me. "You know what that means, don't you?"

"Of course, sir."

Four days had passed since I first saw him, and we'd come to be good friends. Not only did he seem entirely sympathetic to my problems, but he played a mean game of Moopsball, and we'd spent several diverting evenings engaged at the sport.

"Tell me, then. By law I'm required to have absolute proof you and your crew know the law before I release you."

"It means," I said glibly, "that the system is restricted. If we ever return, for any reason, we can be arrested as criminals."

148

"And convicted—don't forget that."

"I haven't, Captain."

"And," he said with a slight smile, "we're putting a restraining order—also Class V—on you and your crew."

"What?" I demanded, hardly able to believe what I'd just heard. "Did you say Class V, sir?"

"Yes. Everyone on board the *Marrow Falcon* is hereby forbidden from mentioning this system to anyone, ever again, until such time as the League decides to reclassify Xelthufed—and you can believe me, they won't until long after you're dead and scattered."

"But why—"

He sighed. "I follow orders, just like you. That's all."

"Surely you have some idea. . . ."

"Yes."

"Tell me, then—captain to captain."

He shook his head. "No. I can't. I'm sorry, Kel. I like you. But I have my job to do, and that comes first. I hope you understand."

I nodded. "Yes, sir. And . . . I want to thank you for not attacking the star-creatures. I thought you would, for a while."

He smiled and relaxed a bit. "Perhaps I might have, if you hadn't cooperated with me and let me communicate with them. You've got the makings of a fine officer. Now get back to your ship, sir. You wanted out of this system as soon as possible. The scientists and political runners will be busy here for the next hundred years, and we're not welcome."

"See you around? Nonprofessionally, of course, sir."

"I wouldn't have it any other way!"

And we both laughed.

THE END

SAVAGE, SAINT, MARTYR

I couldn't let Toff have my equipment. These star-creatures had attacked my ship, plundered the computer's data base, and taken Ghu knew what. They could be planning anything. And—if they truly did have all that information at their disposal—they'd know the capabilities of not only the *Marrow Falcon* but Patrol ships such as the *Vortex Blaster* . . . and how to get around the weapons systems. If they learned they could kill Patrolmen easily, where would they stop?

I couldn't trust Captain Toff not to provoke them. From all the Patrol captains I'd ever met, I knew his type: ambitious, quick to shoot, eager for blood and fighting and promotion. He'd be fast to try to make a name for himself . . . and what better way than provoking an alien race to a showdown and then conquering them (for the good of the League, of course)?

I had my doubts as to whether he'd succeed in defeating the star-creatures—but that was beside the point. If one Patrol ship got destroyed, ten more would replace it. And when they destroyed Xelthufed, an entire sentient race would be lost—and it would be my fault!

No. I couldn't take the chance and turn my data over to Captain Toff. I'd destroy it first.

"Well?" Toff demanded. "I haven't got all year! Surrender your data now, or you'll have to face the consequences."

"Give us a minute, sir," I said. "We're having trouble with the computer."

"Very well." Static crackled from the speaker as he disconnected.

"Sir?" Jamis said. "What should we do?"

"Prepare for nullspace jump," I ordered.

"Course already plotted, sir—to the far side of Xelthufed?"

"Yes. It'll buy us time, if nothing else."

"Aye, sir." He turned back to his console. "There's a window coming up. Should I take it?"

"Yes!"

"Jump time . . . fifteen seconds. Fourteen . . . Thirteen. . . ."

I leaned back and let the computer flash the war tactical grid onto my retina. The *Marrow Falcon* lay in the middle of the series of cubes. The star-creatures still sat at one end and the *Vortex Blaster* still moved at the other . . . and Captain Toff's ship was rapidly closing with mine.

". . . Nine . . . Eight. . . ."

"Computer," I said, sub-vocalizing. "Status?"

"Yes, Captain Corrian. The ship is now prepared for nullspace slip. The nullspace power fields are activated."

". . . Three . . . Two. . . ."

"Prepare to slip—"

". . . One. . . ."

"Now!"

I grew disoriented within the computer's war tact grid field. The criss-crossed grid lines seemed to be turning into themselves, wrapping around into Moebius strips—the effect was something like being trapped in a Klein bottle, looking forward and seeing my back in the distance. I shuddered, vertigo and panic clawing at my thoughts.

Then the war tact grid shimmered and retraced itself, forming back into the familiar cube-pattern. Only now— now the *Marrow Falcon* lay at the far right of the picture. Xelthufed itself filled the center, and at the left extreme floated the star-creatures with the Patrol ship closing on them.

But, rather than remain in one place, the star-creatures now moved. They were withdrawing slowly toward their home star, the glow of their bodies (ships?) stretching out in brilliant white-gold comet-tails, becoming longer. And with their increased size, the fires that had made them shine so brilliantly when they first attacked became somewhat muted and dull, like tarnished silver.

Perhaps, I thought, they've run out of energy and need to return to Xelthufed before they become too cold and die. Or perhaps, with my ship gone from their immediate view, they see no reason to stay any longer.

Whichever—it no longer concerned me. The star-creatures' threat was gone. Captain Barlen Toff remained as my major problem. No doubt I'd made him furious. He'd be out for my blood.

How could I throw him off the scent, get him out of the system? Surely he'd spotted the star-creatures by now! I needed to lure him away. If he didn't file a report on the creatures—and found no way to provoke them—then everyone would probably leave them alone. It might be millennia before our two species contacted one another again . . . if we ever did.

I blinked and put myself back in the control room. "How long till the Patrol ship makes the jump and follows us?" I asked Jamis.

He checked the charts already on the computer-screen. "Minimum time would be at least forty minutes, considering they have to find us, chart the slips, and set-up their power-fields to jump, sir."

I leaned back. "Good. And while they're plotting the course to get here, lay in one to put us back pretty much where we were. A thousand klick deviation should be about right."

"You mean. . . ?"

I grinned. "We can circle the star forever. If the Patrol wants to play games with sovereignty, we'll just disappear for a while."

Tech Oland Plushmir, the gray-skinned Tellonian human who acted as Tech Shucel Baref's relief on the ship's communication equipment, had taken his post while I was absorbed in the computer's war tact grid. He saluted me smartly, and I returned the gesture.

Then he turned back to his controls, studied them, and suddenly tensed.

"What is it?" I demanded.

"Sir, I'm picking up a signal to the Patrol ship. It's coming from the second docking bay . . . from the control room of a Blackmark-model shuttle!"

"Block it, then put the output on my monitor," I snapped, looking down at the screen on the arm of my control chair.

It flickered with white lines and static for an instant, then settled down into a picture—of Tech Shucel Baref. I gaped at her.

". . . star-creatures will be caught. I suspect Captain Corrian to be in the pay of—"

I jabbed the over-ride button and cut her off before she could finish her sentence. Shucel Baref, a Patrol spy! Of all the crewmen aboard, I never would've suspected her! I'd worked with her, played Moopsball with her. I'd even begun to think of her as a friend.

And now she'd betrayed me.

The thought stung. Cutting into her channel, I saw her calm, ice-pale face. Her eyes were dark and unreadable, remote, aloof. She regarded me on her monitor with cold detachment, as though I were a stranger.

"So?" I said, hoping for some kind of explanation.

She said nothing.

I should have Security there with stunguns and wrist-cuffs, but—she was my friend. . . .

"You have three minutes to turn yourself in at the nearest guard station. If you take longer, you'll only make your confinement all the more unpleasant." I couldn't keep the bitterness and disappointment out of my voice.

"Yes, Captain Corrian." No sign of remorse, no emotion. The Patrol trained its people well. Turning, she stalked away from the monitor. I saw her step through the open hatch, then she vanished from my view.

Biting my lip, I looked away. Shucel Baref—she'd been our spy. She'd brought the Patrol down on us. It hurt to think that one of the few people I'd gotten to know well on the *Falcon*—one of the few people I'd really liked—had betrayed me. I sighed, feeling old and tired.

When I punched up the end-level's guard station, a heavily muscled, red-and-black uniformed man with a face scarred from too much exposure to power fields appeared on the monitor. He saluted snappily.

"Yes, Captain?"

"Tech Shucel Baref will turn herself in to you within the next three minutes. She is to be confined and watched closely. The charge is grade 3 mutiny."

"Aye, sir. A spy. Anything else?"

"If she doesn't turn herself in, take a squad of men and go find her. Render her senseless, if she proves uncooperative, but take care not to injure her." I tapped the button and his picture faded from view. Looking over at Oland Plushmir, I said: "Good work."

"Maybe she didn't have time to tell them too much, sir," he said. "She must've planned it all. . . ."

I shrugged, not wanting to think or talk about it anymore. "Just so we stopped her."

"Sir, the *Vortex Blaster*'s engine emissions have

changed," Jamis reported. "The thrusters have stopped. They're drifting free now. Nullspace power fields are charging. . . ."

"Then they've located us."

"Shucel's message must've just reached them. They'll be plotting their nullspace slip now."

"Is our return course computed yet?"

He studied his computer screen. "I'll need five more minutes at least."

"Hurry up, then." I slipped back into the computer's war tact grid.

As I watched, the star-creatures flowed back into their sun and vanished from sight. Then I turned my attention to the *Vortex Blaster*—and, at that very moment, it rippled and vanished from the screen.

"Jamis!" I shouted. "They've slipped!"

Distantly, I heard his voice cry, "I'm not done yet—"

Then the war tact grid dissolved and reformed with a larger scale—the *Vortex Blaster* had reappeared a scant two kilometers astern of my ship. I could see its hundreds of bristling gun-turrets, its dozen docking bays for small fighters, its rows of atomic cannons, all perfect in every detail, all trained on my ship. I swallowed, half-expecting Toff to open fire at once.

"Raise the force shields!" I called. An instant later, a white halo surrounded the image of the *Marrow Falcon* on the war tact grid.

The intercom crackled, then I heard the familiar voice of Captain Toff once more.

"Captain Corrian, I'm rapidly losing patience. This is your last chance to cooperate. Truly, you will have no other."

I knew he was sincere. One didn't get a Patrol captain mad and expect him just to roll over and play dead like some Arcturan bunny. I just wanted to buy Jamis more time. We had to get away. . . .

"Very well, Corrian. Your last chance has just passed. There will be no other."

Just then, all the control room lights went out at once. For a minute, all of us floated silently in the pitch-darkness of the cabin. Even the intercom had failed. It was a tense, frightening moment. I felt the claustrophobia begin to work on me. One of the techs screamed, a sharp, primal sound.

"Jamis!" I shouted.

From somewhere to my left. "Sir!"

"What the devil happened? Get some lights on! We're going to have to fight if we don't slip!"

With a growl of returning power, about half the emergency lights came on. By their red glow, I made a quick survey of the control room. Almost all of the techs had floated away from their duty stations, shock and bewilderment apparent on their faces, and most of the view-screens remained dark, or filled with static. What had happened?

"Get back to your posts, damn it!" I shouted.

They grabbed rungs in the walls and pulled themselves back to the consoles. Within a minute, the rest of the lights went on.

"Hurry up, Jamis," I said, trying to maintain my control.

"Sir," someone called frantically, "the computers are still down!"

Then the in-ship intercom beeped. I jabbed the button. "What?"

"Captain." A uniformed First Guard was on the screen. He saluted me. "The power loss was sabotage. We caught Second Tech Shucel Baref in the power room. She's now being restrained in a holding tank. They're trying to repair the damage now, sir."

I had a sinking feeling in the pit of my stomach. "How much damage, and how long will it take to fix?"

"Full electricity will be restored to the ship in a matter of minutes, sir. The nullspace power fields have completely collapsed and the techs say they need at least twenty minutes to reenergize them—and even then we'd be slipping blind. Most of the damage was centered around the computer banks—the whole inside works are going to have to be rewired, even just to access data, and that's going to take several hours."

"Damn. Keep me posted."

His image winked out.

Leaning back, I tried to slip into the war tact grid—and found nothing there. The computers were completely down. I couldn't get access to the weapons, or the data banks, or the guidance system to bring the ship through nullspace. We were trapped where we were. If the power-fields were fully energized, we could conceivably make a slip into nullspace, but we'd be travelling blind, unable to plot a course . . . and thus likely to strike a star, or planet, or just get lost so far from known space that we'd never get home. Blind slips were the last resort of a desperate captain—the thing you did if your vessel was about to be destroyed. I knew the *Vortex Blaster* wouldn't destroy us—they didn't have to now.

I couldn't even dump the information I had on the star-creatures. The *Marrow Falcon* had become one of those legendary terrestrial oysters, ready for the plucking, feathers and all. We lay completely at Captain Toff's mercy.

Swearing softly, cursing myself for being a sentimental idiot and not placing Shucel under arrest at once, I opened a channel to Toff's ship. "This is Captain Corrian. I wish to speak to Captain Toff."

"Regarding?" a man's voice inquired.

I swallowed. "Negotiations for the surrender of my ship."

It was settled quickly.

"Captain Corrian," said Captain Toff, "I'm going to allow you to keep nominal command of the *Marrow Falcon*, but your powers will be severely limited. All instructions to your crew will come through me. Keep them in their quarters when off-duty, and have them obey my men when they come aboard."

"That sounds fair, sir," I said, and I meant it. In fact, it was more than I'd expected. By all rights, Toff should've stripped me of my command and locked me up in his ship's brig. After all, disobeying a Patrol captain's direct orders violated a half-dozen League laws. But perhaps he had reasons for trying to win my cooperation, rather than force it through bullying.

"Good, I'm glad you agree to my terms. Your force shield is down, and make sure it stays down. My ship is maneuvering into position to link up with yours. Prepare to receive boarders."

"Very well, sir."

But static already hissed over the intercom—he'd switched his end off. I shut mine down as well, leaning back with a sigh as I did so. All told, things hadn't gone as badly as I'd expected.

Then the ship lurched to the right, and I felt an odd tugging sensation in my left side, as though a slight gravity pulled me in that direction. Toff had activated his ship's tractor beams, I knew, and our two vessels were slowly being pulled together.

I flipped open my in-ship intercom to address my crew. "This is Captain Corrian speaking," I said. "Due to sabotage by a Patrol spy, I've been forced to relinquish com-

mand of our ship to the Patrol. I expect all crew members
to cooperate fully with the Patrol officers and soldiers who
come aboard."

As expected, before I finished the announcement, the
Ship's Council was calling me. I punched the intercom
button and Vimister Groll's face filled the small
viewscreen on the arm of my chair.

"Captain Corrian," he said, face grave, "what's the
meaning of this?"

"I thought it was obvious," I said tiredly. "Rather than
let the ship be destroyed, I surrendered. It was a choice of
life or death—I assumed you'd want me to choose life.
There wasn't time to consult you, so I made the decision
myself. That's my job."

"For the time being," he said, "if things work out. Be
warned: I don't approve of your decision, nor do the other
Council members. It may well prove to be grounds for
your dismissal!"

"I'll take that chance," I said. "I have faith in my ability."

He frowned. "So did the *Falcon*'s last commander. She
didn't listen to Council decisions and tried to run the ship
as though we didn't exist."

"What happened?"

He shrugged and signed off.

I swallowed. Free Traders could be merciless if pushed
too far. Their ships, their businesses, were everything.
Shivering slightly, I shut off the intercom.

"Captain," Jamis said, "the computer scanner just
came on—it's showing a picture now, and I think you better take a look."

"Very well." Leaning back, I slipped into the war tact
grid, which was a part of the scanning system. The cube
pattern had reformed once again, and I looked out on Xel-

thufed and our two ships that seemed to be almost touching now. Then I noticed three odd, glowing shapes moving out from Xelthufed—more star-creatures. And they were headed straight toward us.

What were they up to this time? Just watching? Or something more violent, now that they'd scouted out the *Falcon*'s weaknesses?

Now I knew why Captain Toff had been so eager to win my ship without a fight—it looked like he might have a real battle on his hands in a matter of moments.

I tried to swallow and found my throat achingly dry. Snapping out of the grid, I flipped open the intercom between my ship and the *Vortex Blaster*. This time, Captain Toff spoke to me immediately.

"Captain Corrian." His voice was cold, professional, like a hired killer's. "I imagine you've noticed by now that some objects have left Xelthufed."

"Yes, sir. That's why I called. What are you going to do about it?"

"Is there some cause for alarm, Captain? I thought you implied this wasn't a military situation?"

He's baiting me! I thought, taking instant offense at his tone. Damn it, if he wanted to know something, why didn't he just come out and ask? With the star-creatures coming, I didn't have time to play his little games, and I suspected he didn't have that much time, either.

Suddenly an idea came to me. I'd get him to retreat—take him away from the aliens. That way he wouldn't be able to provoke them to a fight. Quickly I said, "Yes, there's a 'cause for alarm'— those are aliens who're coming! Now what're you going to do about it? My ship's in your protective custody—remember that. Now protect us!"

"I'll take care of them—that's what the *Vortex Blaster* is

for."

"That's not what I mean, sir! You'll have to give us an escort out of this system. It might turn into a battlefield, and we're civilians. League laws say—"

"League laws say I don't have to do that if the threat can be eliminated. And I can eliminate it."

"You can't make an unprovoked attack—"

"It was provoked. They attacked your ship first."

"We're not sure of that—"

"I am. Don't worry, Corrian, the Patrol's here now. We'll take good care of you." A sneer crept into his voice now, as though he were talking to a child and his patience had just run out. "This ship's a match for anything in the galaxy."

"You must withdraw from the system!"

"I don't run from a fight."

"Then—then at least try to communicate with them!"

He gave a short, barking laugh. "How? Our two life-forms have nothing in common. How could we possibly talk to them? Are you some miracle linguist?"

"No, of course not. But one of my first techs managed to hook up a device that let us communicate with them. It worked pretty well—"

"You should have told me this earlier, Corrian! I don't want war anymore than you do! Show my men where it is—immediately. They'll transfer it to my ship."

I sighed. "Yes, Captain, I'll tell your men where it is."

"Do so." He disconnected.

I tried to think of another alternative—anything to get Captain Toff to leave the star-creatures alone—but couldn't think of a single thing. It seemed as though everything I'd tried to accomplish had come out wrong—the star-creatures attacking, Shucel Baref betraying me, Captain Toff taking control of my ship. I had one last thing to do—I had to prevent Toff from fighting with the aliens. Oh, he'd said he didn't want war, but if he meant it, he'd be the *first* Patrol captain I'd ever met who felt that way!

Oland Plushmir interrupted my thoughts. "Captain Corrian, several of the techs Captain Toff sent over are demanding to know where the communication equipment is kept. What should I tell them, sir?"

"The truth—in the laboratory on the third level, room 84."

He repeated what I'd said.

"Where are the star-creatures now?" I asked Jamis urgently.

He studied the screen before him. "They've stopped moving. They're almost two hundred kilometers away, directly between our ship and Xelthufed. Sir . . . it's as though they're trying to block our way. We can't return to the star without going through them first."

"Interesting," I said. But it didn't help much.

The in-ship intercom suddenly beeped. I jumped, startled, then pushed the button. Luathek's image filled the screen. "What is it?"

"Kel," the Pavian wailed, "they are taking the equipment from the laboratory! They are ripping it out from the walls and floor with no regards for the damages!"

"Let them," I said. "There's nothing I can do. We're under the Patrol's jurisdiction now, and we'll have to live with their terrorism."

Much as it pained me, I severed the connection. When I filed my report with the League, I'd have a lot to say about Captain Toff . . . none of it good.

An hour later, after Captain Toff's men had forcibly removed the communication equipment from my ship, Oland called to me.

I slipped out of the war tact grid where I'd been studying the position of the star-creatures. They hadn't moved for a long, long time.

"What's happening?" I asked him.

"I'm picking up a low-band signal from Captain Toff's ship. I think it's translatable back into Basic. . . . Yes! I've got it now."

"Put it on my monitor."

"Yes, sir."

Toff: . . . at once. I won't tolerate threats!

Other: . . . Kill. . . . You go or we will kill. . . . Kill.

Toff: My ship is more than a match for any weapons you have. I order you to return to your home.

Other: . . . GO.

Toff: I am under the authority of the League of Planets! Obey me!

Other: Kill . . . you . . . planets. . . .

Toff: You continue to threaten the League. You refuse to listen to reason. I have only one choice, by League law—I must remove your threat. This is your last chance. Surrender now, or the consequences will be disastrous.

Other: . . . Kill.

Toff: So be it.

I shivered. My worst fears had come to pass—Captain Toff was going to attack the star-creatures! Punching the intercom button, I found, didn't accomplish anything. Preparing for battle, the *Vortex Blaster* ignored my signal.

The ship shuddered around me. I froze, bewildered, wondering what had happened.

"They've released the tractor beams, Captain," Jamis called. "Their weapons systems are powering up."

The ship shuddered a second time, and, suddenly, alarms began to go off.

"Ship under attack, Captain Corrian," the computer

said in my ear.

I slipped into the computer net and the option screen rose before me:

STATUS REPORT AS FOLLOWS:

1) SHIP'S ENGINES SUFFERED DIRECT
   LOW-POWER HIT BY ENERGY CANNON.

2) REPAIRS UNDER WAY: ESTIMATED
   COMPLETION TIME IS TWO HOURS.
   NEW ORDERS?

"None for now, apparently," I said, cursing softly to myself. Apparently, Captain Toff shot my engines to keep me from leaving while he dealt with the star-creatures.

I called up the computer's external hologram and the air in front of me shimmered, rippling as though with heat waves. There, against a field of darkness, I saw the *Marrow Falcon* and the *Vortex Blaster*. They'd drifted a bit apart. Suddenly, the *Blaster*'s engines flamed to life, and it moved toward the star-creatures at the far right of the hologram.

"Track that ship."

"Yes, Captain Corrian," the computer responded.

An incessant beeping sound nagged at me. I looked down. The Ship's Council was calling.

I pushed the button. "What?" I snapped. I didn't have time for their complaints. A ripple of tension and fear passed through my body as I thought of the *Vortex Baster* attacking the star-creatures.

"Corrian, what do you think you're doing?" Ulega Max demanded.

"I don't have time now."

"You'd better make time. Corrian, we think—"

I punched the button, shutting him off. The instant I did, the intercom began to beep again. Ignoring it, I watched the hologram, knowing they'd reprimand me later—but whatever they wanted now couldn't possibly be as important as what was going on outside.

I saw the *Vortex Blaster* moving closer and closer to the aliens. The ship's atomic cannons swivelled, locking onto their targets. A force shield shimmered around the whole vessel. Still it advanced at a steady pace.

The star-creatures seemed unaware of the threat. They maintained their position between the *Blaster* and Xel-thufed, unmoving, silent.

Brilliant stripes of light shot from the ship's gun turrets. Balls of glowing energy hurled from the cannons. I held my breath as the hologram flickered with light for a second.

Then the image cleared, and I gasped in shock. Where the energy bolts had hit the star-creatures, nothing had happened! The aliens might've glowed a bit brighter, but that was it. They appeared completely unharmed. I wouldn't have thought it possible for any ship or life-form to withstand such a brutal attack unshielded, and my respect for the star-creatures went up several notches. They were, indeed, a force to be feared.

I continued to stare, open-mouthed, as Captain Toff's ship fired a second time, then a third—with equal effect. The star-creatures couldn't be hurt, not by Toff's weapons at least.

For an instant, I felt overwhelmed with relief. I wouldn't be responsible for a war after all! At last, something had worked out. Then my pleasure turned to shock as the star-creatures began to move. They glowed with a brilliant white light, like suns gone nova, and their bodies began to expand. Long, thin tendrils extended from their sides like hundreds of cilia, growing longer and longer until they reached thousands of meters in length. Finally, nothing remained of their amoeboid form; all three star-creatures had become writhing masses of white tendrils.

They moved toward the still-advancing *Vortex Blaster* like an army of snakes. At the last second, Toff's ship tried to veer to the left, but the star-creatures caught up with it anyway.

They passed through the force shield like knives through butter, then passed through the hull like ghosts—and then they were gone, completely vanished from view. I stared at the *Vortex Blaster*, a cold, uncomfortable lump in the middle of my stomach. I could imagine the star-creatures racing through the corridors, burning the controls, ravaging the computers, destroying the equipment.

Then the Patrol ship exploded—not as in old movies, with great rushes of flame and loud sounds—but as starships truly explode. There was a quick flash of light, then one side of the *Blaster* burst open and jets of air and water spurted out. The vapor froze almost instantly, and the ice crystals formed a brilliant rainbow across the dark tapestry of stars. In space, there is beauty in death.

Then the fusion reactor went next, and a series of brilliant blue-white flashes almost blinded me. Waves of energy spread out from the wrecked ship like rings in a pool.

Nothing remained on the holograph but the three star-creatures. They'd become amoeba-shaped again, drifting apart until they'd resumed their positions between the *Marrow Falcon* and Xelthufed. They moved neither forward nor back, but floated there, waiting.

I was more than a little surprised that they made no

effort to attack us. After all, to them we must've appeared just as guilty. Then it occurred to me that they'd only destroyed Toff's ship because he'd fired directly on them. They appeared content just to ward us off. I was grateful for my own prudence in not attacking them—it had probably saved my ship.

I guessed then that the star-creatures' first trip through the *Falcon* had been nothing more than a warning, a quick look around and a display of power. They truly did want us to leave—and were willing to let us go, even after the *Vortex Blaster* tried to kill them.

I leaned back in my seat, suddenly weak. My adrenaline rush was over, now that the danger seemed past. Finding myself soaked with sweat, I wiped my brow with my sleeve. Captain Toff was dead. All his crewmen were dead. It was a cold, harsh, unexpected blow.

There would certainly be a war now, when the Patrol found out. If only . . . If only Toff had listened to me in the first place. If only the star-creatures hadn't destroyed his ship. If only . . .

I sighed. Toff had done a pretty good job of disabling my ship; but the engines would soon be repaired.

Perhaps the Patrol didn't have to find out what happened. We'd be long-gone before the *Vortex Blaster*'s reinforcements arrived. I knew that, if they found us here, they'd quarantine the system, seize the *Falcon*, and interrogate me and my crew for endless long hours. We'd be lucky to get away at all, if they suspected we knew something we weren't telling.

And I knew they'd nova Xelthufed "to eliminate the menace of hostile aliens."

No, it was best to leave. Best for the star-creatures, best for me and my ship. Toff wouldn't care one way or another.

I called my repair techs. "Hurry up with the engines," I said. "We haven't got all day."

Then I called the Ship's Council. I had a lot of explaining to do—

THE END

BLOOD JEWELS

I decided to help Ulega Max. After all, if he and his crew really were in some sort of danger, I couldn't just leave them to die. And if they weren't, I'd make them pay. The Courts had no great fondness for Free Traders to begin with, and Free Traders who broadcast fake distress calls . . . I knew we'd have no trouble winning a law suit.

"Very well," I said slowly. "We'll help you. But you'll have to tell me what the problem is before I can do anything."

He shook his head. "Approach the *Falcon* slowly. You'll see what's going on—and be able to help us accordingly. And . . . thank you, Captain Corrian, for agreeing. You and your crew will be suitably rewarded." Then the viewscreen grew dark.

I sat back, puzzled by his words. What could be so dangerous—and so important to him—that it couldn't be discussed over an open channel? His behavior had been very odd, to say the least. If nothing else, I planned to investigate just to satisfy my own curiosity.

"Change course for the *Marrow Falcon*," I said. "Scan ahead and see if there's anything in the immediate area surrounding her—another ship, perhaps, or debris of any kind."

"Aye, sir," all the techs said. They bent over their equipment and set to work eagerly. The monitors hummed. Numbers flashed on the viewscreens, marking various system coordinates as they checked them.

I slipped back into the navigational screen, studying our progress. We closed with the *Falcon* at a steady rate. We'd be able to dock within the hour, if that's what Ulega wanted. Finally, I slipped from the screen to see if my techs had found anything yet.

"Sir," called Kagan, the small, soft-spoken woman in charge of adjusting nullspace power fields. I glanced down at the system monitors built into the arm of my command chair and noted that she'd been scanning the space directly around the *Marrow Falcon*.

"What's there?"

"I . . . don't quite know, sir. I'm picking up three blips on my screen. They're radiating energy on all wavelengths. There's also a small area of magnetic disturbance around them, like solar turbulence. Only that's impossible—isn't it, Captain?"

"I don't know," I said. "There are more things in space than we can ever imagine. Perhaps this is one of the so-called 'impossible phenomena' scientists are always talking about."

She jerked upright. "Sir, those blips—they're moving! They're closing in on the *Falcon*, surrounding her."

"What?" I demanded. Leaning back, I called up the computer's war tact grid. The air before me flickered, then the grid appeared. It picked data up from all the ship's scanners, providing a three-dimensional hologram of the space surrounding my ship. The *Trim Dreamer* moved in the center of the picture; the *Marrow Falcon* occupied the far left side.

The "disturbances" appeared as glowing amoeboid shapes. As I watched, they moved forward and took up positions around the *Falcon*. Strings of light shot from one to another, connecting them, forming a huge web—with Ulega Max's starship caught like an insect in its center. The web glowed, the vacuum fairly pulsed with energy.

"Those strings of light are a controlled form of power, sir!" Kagan called, shocked. "They're being manipulated like tools—it's as though the blips are sentients!"

The idea shocked me. If those amoeboid shapes were intelligent creatures, that would explain Ulega Max's insistence on secrecy—it meant the *Falcon* had stumbled on a new type of life . . . a whole new intelligent race. If they could work out some sort of exclusive treaty, set up trade with the creatures, they'd have a trade monopoly. A very profitable trade monopoly. No wonder he didn't want me to find out what they were really up to.

But the natives seemed hostile, and probably had no intention of cooperating with Ulega Max's little plan. I chuckled. They appeared to be defending themselves quite well—even on the hologram I could see that the *Falcon*'s weapon ports had all been sealed shut. The hull around them had been melted to slag. The ship lay defenseless.

I wondered, briefly, what had happened to the Blackmark-model shuttles. Their four berths were empty; no trace remained of them.

It seemed Ulega and his crew had gotten themselves in over their heads . . . and it was up to me to set things straight. And I'd make sure they paid enough royals to make this rescue well worth my effort and the time we were losing!

"Sir," Rooli Tebwah said, from her communications console. "Ulega Max is screaming for you on channel one."

I punched him up on my chair's viewscreen. Tebwah hadn't exaggerated. Max was, indeed, screaming. His face was white and he appeared to be trembling. The picture wavered and threatened to dissolve at any moment—due to the interference caused by the creatures, I knew. Then the image locked firmly into place and I knew Ulega's people had switched to a tight-beam transmission.

"Corrian—we need you here at once! They've

171

breached the hull in two places! The computer systems are burning out. Hurry!"

"I want a deal first," I said, knowing that, no matter what he asked, the *Trim Dreamer* could not get there any sooner; we were already moving at full thrust and couldn't go faster than that in realspace. From the war tact grid's display, we'd be in range to use our weapons in about a minute, but Ulega Max wouldn't realize that. Making deals like this was common Free Trader practice, I knew. They never missed a chance to turn a profit—and neither would I.

"What deal?" he said. His voice was suddenly cold. "What do you want?"

"I know what your ship's doing here."

"That's impossible."

I smiled. "It's pretty obvious. And I want a share in exchange for the use of this ship. Say . . . fifty percent of the gross profits?"

"Never!" he snarled. "We'll die first, Corrian!" Then came the sound of an explosion. The lights behind him flickered and went out for a second, but emergency power came on. By its dim illumination, his face seemed gray. Stress-lines made him look decades older than he really was.

"Okay!" he shouted. "I'll give you ten percent, net profits—but you'll have to do some of the work. Now hurry!"

I said nothing. Glancing at the war tact grid, I noted the time and began powering up the weapons systems. Twenty seconds. . . .

He gasped, looking over his shoulder. Sweat rolled down his cheeks. "Corrian, be reasonable—"

I said, "Thirty percent, net. Consider us overhead."

"Fifteen!"

"Twenty-five."

Ten seconds. . . .

"Eighteen! Corrian—please!"

Shrugging, I suggested, "Twenty-two?"

"Nineteen—I can't do better than that!"

"I could always wait and claim your whole ship as salvage," I said, making my voice sound as if I watched ships blow up every day, just for amusement. "Twenty?"

"Done!" he shouted.

One second. . . .

I slipped entirely into the war tact grid. The weapons systems locked onto my retinas, following the movement of my eyes. There were advantages to captaining an old Patrol ship, I realized—the weapons were the best money could buy. I focused on the nearest creature, locked in an atomic missile, and ordered, "Fire!"

A white line streaked across the grid. When it was within a half kilometer of the *Falcon*, I detonated it. A white sphere, rapidly expanding, marked its position as waves of energy radiated out. Atomics could be pretty messy, but I'd set this one off far enough away from the *Marrow Falcon* that her screens could deal with the excess radiation. Nobody inside would be harmed.

Still, I didn't expect the reaction it got. The creatures leaped away from the *Falcon* as if burned, leaving the white web of power lines to slowly dissipate. They must've been moving near the speed of sound—they zipped across the grid almost faster than I could follow, plunged into Beta Dainis—that red giant star—and disappeared from sight.

I literally blinked and they were gone. It had been easy—too easy, I thought.

I'd suspected, when Kagan said they seemed to be generating power fields, that an atomic detonation might scramble their internal structures, just as it would damage power fields on a planet, but I had no way of testing the idea. Apparently, it had worked. I sighed, pleased with the result. And I knew Jawn Kessel would be pleased with the deal I'd made. Twenty percent of another ship's profits—for doing almost nothing!

Ulega Max could still be seen on the intercom's viewscreen, but he was no longer looking into the monitor. Instead, he was calling orders to the crew, sending them scurrying around the control room, repairing damage and charting a new course for his ship.

I cleared my throat. He heard me and turned.

"Captain Corrian," he said. "You're still there."

"I need to protect my ship's money," I said.

"Perhaps you'd better come over to the *Falcon*. We can discuss the matter in a more . . . civil manner. I have to convene the Ship's Council."

"Do so, then. I'll take a shuttle over and meet you in—an hour from now." I'd give him time to get himself cleaned up and his ship organized before meeting a new partner.

"Use the third docking bay. I'll see you shortly."

Switching off the viewscreen, I leaned back and grinned. I was even starting to think like a Free Trader!

The airlock cycled and I stepped into the *Falcon*'s huge loading bay.

I'd changed into a bright green and gold dress uniform, with polished black boots and white gloves—putting on the whole show for the crew of the *Marrow Falcon* . . . and her Ship's Council. I walked forward, flanked by two guards from my ship, and headed toward the waiting delegation. I pretended aloofness, but studied all around me.

The loading bay was almost deserted. My footsteps

echoed around me, a lonely, desolate sound. Huge blue and white plastithane crates had been stacked along the far wall, and various loading equipment had been parked in small stalls to my left, but other than that the place looked all but unused. Repellers set at regular intervals across the high ceiling provided a pleasant pseudo-gravity, about half a gee.

I recognized Ulega Max and Jespar Melsif—both in slick black dress uniforms—waiting for me, plus four black-and-red uniformed guards, who carried heavy blasters strapped to their legs. Several guards wore double-helix medallions in plain sight—it was obvious they'd been preparing to die until I showed up.

"The greetings of my ship's owner and myself," I said, inclining my head slightly. The guards behind me halted.

"And ours to you." Ulega returned the salute. With authority restored to his ship, much of his bruskness had returned. I found I still didn't trust him—or like him.

"Time is money," I said. "I'll see your Ship's Council now."

"As you wish. Please follow." Then he turned and started forward, toward a small lift at the far end of the loading bay. His men fell in step around us, and I had the strangest sensation of being a prisoner rather than an honored guest. I didn't like the feeling.

At last we reached the passenger lift. It was small, designed to hold no more than two people at a time, but I managed to squeeze in alongside Ulega and Melsif. Their guards waited silently as we descended into the heart of the ship.

"I'll be back soon," I promised my men. They nodded, but they wore grim expressions. They obviously didn't like me going anywhere with Max alone.

Thinking about that, I turned to Ulega Max, who was

busy pretending I didn't exist. "How long will this take?"

"Not long, I should imagine." He shrugged. "Not long."

At last, the lift stopped and we all squeezed out into a high, wide corridor. The deck beneath our feet was made of plastithane grating. It stretched far right and left, slowly curving out of sight. The walls were featureless and gray. Overhead, repellers and light panels had been set in a monotonous, repeating pattern. Unmarked doors opened to either side.

"This way." Ulega turned to the left. I hurried to keep step with him, and Jespar Melsif brought up the rear. When we reached a large gold-painted door with a red double-helix symbol blaxed across its middle, he touched the handpad and it slid open at once.

A single table had been set up within, and behind it stood three cushioned chairs. In two of them sat old men with faces scarred from long years' exposure to nullspace power fields. Ulega Max moved forward and sat in the third seat. After linking his fingers and placing them under his chin, he leaned forward and studied me for a long second. I tried not to shift uncomfortably beneath his gaze.

"Well?" I finally demanded.

"This is the Ship's Council," he said. "I present Senior Traders Vimister Groll and Yamal Hydrif."

The two old men nodded.

"I'm most pleased to meet you," I said.

"I've already told them of the agreement you forced me to make," Ulega Max said. "Now that you're going to be our partner—whether we like it or not—it's time you found out what we're really doing in this system."

"I think that's obvious," I said. "You're trying to open trade relations with those star-creatures. You want a trade monopoly."

Ulega smiled thinly, as though tolerating an idiot. "Hardly that."

"What, then?" I demanded. "There's nothing else here!"

Vimister Groll leaned forward, stroking his chin pensively. "It's this way, lad, and you'd better cotton to my words, if you don't want to be shivved in the end, fer sure."

I stared at him, bewildered. "What language is this?" I asked, wondering if I'd need a translator.

Ulega Max sighed. "He says he wants you to listen to him."

Groll smiled. "It's cool. My hobby is old Earth vids . . . and, I must admit, I do have the unfortunate habit of picking up their primitive slingo. Please—if I appear not to be making sense, just tell me and I'll try to talk more colloquially."

"All right," I said cautiously. "You were telling me why you brought your ship to such a back-water system as Beta Dainis."

"To mine jewels."

I snorted derisively. "But there's nothing here to mine— not even an asteroid belt! You might as well try to extract fresh fruit from the vacuum."

"Do you really think so?" He drew a small cloth bag from one pocket, opened it, and spilled out—a handful of sunlight.

I gaped. It took me a minute to realize he held a dozen finely cut and polished jewels . . . and what jewels! In every facet hung a miniature star, the gems seemed to shine with a light of their own. When I tried to estimate their worth on the open market, I knew they'd bring phenomenal prices. The old man held a dozen fortunes in his hand. With such gems, I could buy my own ship, set myself up for life as an independent trader.

Swallowing, I managed to say, "They're beautiful."

"Yes. Beautiful." He slipped them back into the bag. "That's what we're mining—or were trying to mine, until those creatures showed up and put a nix on the process."

"Tell me what happened."

Ulega Max said, "This is the second system we've tried to mine. At the first one, after we'd run a test-skim, creatures similar to the ones here attacked us. We retreated, then slipped here—we weren't looking for a fight.

"When we started over again, we sent in two shuttles to scoop up super-heated hydrogen, which we process into the jewels you saw. The star-creatures destroyed the craft, then moved forward and took up positions just off our bow. Captain Yoonlag tried to drive them off with the other two shuttles, but the creatures attacked and destroyed those two shuttles as well. Then they moved in on us—and that's when you arrived."

"And now we've got twenty percent of whatever you manage to mine?"

"Unfortunate for us, but true," Groll said.

"Well . . . what now?"

"The answer seems obvious," Vimister Groll said. "Since—whether we like it or not—you've become our partner, we think you might as well become a full worker in the starskimming process. Of course, this would mean your ship's getting a full split of the profits, rather than just twenty percent. We feel it's a fair offer, considering your position."

"And what's that?"

"We've got the know-how to skim the fringe atmosphere off stars, but we need equipment—your ship's shuttles would do nicely, for a start. Also, the *Falcon*'s pretty well laid-up. Most of our maintenance techs are dead now. Yours would be a major help in getting her back in shape again. We need you if we're going to process the hydrogen here. You need us if you're going to get a full share in the jewels. What better partnership could there be?"

"I must consult the ship's owner," I said.

Max frowned. "No. If you do not accept our offer, we prefer that you leave immediately and say nothing of this to anyone. If our secret gets out—" He shrugged. "I realize it means we will have to trust you, but there is no help for that. Besides, it is your investment you will be protecting by keeping quiet. Make your decision. Your owner will go along with it, I'm certain."

I hesitated. Twenty percent for doing nothing—or fifty for working. It was a difficult choice. I remembered the jewels Vimister Groll had held . . . how they'd shone with an internal light. That extra thirty percent might be as great a fortune as any independent trade ship ever made— or getting involved might be the biggest mistake of my career. But what if the star-creatures returned? Would I be able to drive them off a second time?

I decided to join up with the *Marrow Falcon* and mine Beta Dainis. Those jewels are just too valuable to pass up! From my share of the *Trim Dreamer*'s income, I'll soon be able to buy a ship of my own . . . something I've always wanted. *Turn to page 184.*

Too risky. I'll keep my twenty percent share of their profits and go on with the work I was hired to do. Mining stars sounds dangerous. I'd rather be alive and working than rich but dead. *Turn to page 194.*

FAST YEARS

I shook my head sadly. "No, Ulega, I can't possibly agree to help you—not if you won't tell me what's wrong. It's not a decision I make lightly, but—I have to think of my own ship. You understand."

"Oh, I understand, all right." He sneered. "You're abandoning another ship in need of help. You're a fool, Corrian, and I'll see you brought up before the League on charges—"

I punched the viewscreen button, cutting him off. An empty threat. The League would back me all the way on this one. For all I knew, he was a pirate luring me into a deadly trap.

The navigational screen still held the coordinates for the next nullspace window—the one that would bring us to the Bronson Alpha system—and I transferred them into the ship's computer. The course locked into place.

"Prepare for nullspace slip," I said.

"Aye, sir," the techs called, as the gauge counted down the seconds. Three . . . two . . . one. . . .

"Slip . . . now." And all the colors in the room began to blur and shift as we left realspace. In thirty-six hours we'd emerge fourteen light-years away, near a small yellow star with four planets.

It would be an uneasy trip for me, as I pondered Ulega Max's words over and over again. I hated the decision he'd forced me to make. If only he'd told me about the problem—

A sparkling blue-green planet hung on the viewscreen, soft whorls of clouds alternately hiding and revealing its surface. Duane's World, with its seven large continents,

hundreds of small interlocking seas, delicate white ice-caps
. . . all things considered, one of the most beautiful planets
ever discovered. A dozen-odd moons circled the planet,
playing strange games with its tides, giving it an oddly sur-
real appearance from space.

I switched my viewscreen to one of the planet's many
communications channel. Instantly, the gray-furred face
of a female Jurisnac appeared. She rubbed her snout with
one hand, then barked a low greeting in Basic.

"Thank you," I said. "Your planet's more beautiful
than I'd heard."

"Is this your first time here?" she asked.

"Yes."

"Then be sure to see the botanical gardens in Diane
City. They're the most amazing spectacle you'll have ever
seen on-planet."

"Thanks," I said. "I'll do that. But now I've got a serious problem. Can you connect me with the Patrol station,
please?"

"Certainly." Her image winked out and, in seconds, the
gold and black star-and-sword emblem of the Patrol
appeared on the screen, along with a "Please Wait" message. It was just like them to keep a Citizen waiting . . . a
form of the psychological intimidation in which the Patrol
specialized. At last the emblem screen grew dark and an
officer's face appeared. He was human, with short-
cropped black hair and slate gray eyes. His mouth had a
hard set.

"Patrol headquarters, Commander Zalpev speaking,"
he said. "What can I do for you, Captain Corrian?"

"You know me?" I asked, surprised.

"The Patrol makes it its business to know everything."

I smiled grimly. "I wish to report a distress call. I
received it in the Beta Dainis system—it came from the

Free Trader ship the *Marrow Falcon*."

"Why didn't you answer it yourself?"

"I would've, but they refused to tell me what was wrong—only that they needed help."

"A correct decision," Commander Zalpev said, sounding surprised that I had that much sense. "Such matters are best left to the Patrol. We've been monitoring the *Marrow Falcon*'s activities for some time. Thank you for notifying us immediately, Captain. We'll take care of the matter. Do not trouble yourself further."

Then the viewscreen went blank and static hissed from the speaker. He'd disconnected.

Secure in the knowledge that the Patrol would take care of everything, I felt completely at ease for the first time in the last two days.

Over the next week, I spent most of my time having the *Trim Dreamer*'s cargo of bayafruit unloaded and shipped to various distribution centers across the planet. I agreed to take a full shipment of Dozois' Hydro-wheat to New Australia, and the profit from that deal put my ship firmly in the black for the year. During the few spare hours I allowed myself, I toured the vast botanical gardens in Diane's City with Luathek. That and my work kept me too busy to worry about the *Marrow Falcon* and her crew. But, on the day before we were scheduled to leave, curiosity got the better of me and I visited the Patrol headquarters.

At the information desk, I found a Centaxi on duty. Its cilia writhed as it asked, "May I help you, Citizen?"

"I'd like to see Commander Zalpev, if possible," I said.

"He is in the first room down the hallway to your left."

"Thanks," I said. I walked down the hall and turned into the first office. Commander Zalpev sat behind a large plastic desk, writing some sort of report on his computer. He pushed the terminal aside when he saw me.

"What can the Patrol do for you today, Captain Corrian?" he asked.

"I was wondering about the *Marrow Falcon*. . . ."

He shook his head. "I'm sorry, but I have no information to give you. Is that all?"

I nodded. "Yes."

"I'm sorry I can't be of help. Good day, Captain." He turned back to his computer. Reluctantly, I went back to my ship.

Over the next few months, whenever the *Trim Dreamer* made planetfall, I'd stop into the local Patrol office and ask about Ulega Max and his ship. Strangely, nobody knew anything—or, if they did, they wouldn't tell me. It was as though the *Falcon* had completely disappeared from the universe, never to be seen again.

Then, in my frustration, I'd go to a tavern with Luathek, drink a silent toast to Ulega Max and his crew, and wonder about what might have been . . . if only I'd had the courage to answer his distress call.

THE END

THE *FALCON* WOUNDED

I decided to join up with the *Falcon*—the money they offered was just too great to pass up. Those jewels. . . . I found myself remembering their every line and facet, their fire and sparkle. Undoubtedly, one of the most beautiful things I'd seen in the universe. I knew without a doubt that Jawn Kessel would agree to my decision to give up our trade route. He simply had to. I longed for jewels like Vimister Groll's with a desperateness that would've amazed and bewildered everyone around me.

But, wisely, I pretended to think it over for a long time. Finally, when the entire Ship's Council began to shift uneasily in their chairs, I knew the time had come. I slowly nodded.

"All right," I said calmly. "I accept your deal—the *Trim Dreamer*'s shuttles will be at your disposal as soon as we work out certain problems."

"Problems?" Ulega Max demanded. "What problems?"

"For one, those star-creatures. Do you really want them attacking us every time we skim Beta Dainis?"

He had to admit he didn't. "But they're no problem— you chased them off easily enough. You can do it again if they come back."

"You're not thinking it through," I said. "Do you want to fight whenever you send the shuttles in? Of course not. I have no intention of running a perpetual war. That's why we're going to have to move to a different star."

Vimister Groll nodded. "I do believe that's a nifty idea! What's the name of the nearest uninhabited star?"

Yamal Hydrif said, "It's Adverton."

"I'm not familiar with it," I said dubiously.

"It's not far from here—about seven light-years—and it doesn't have any planets. Just one asteroid belt. It's closer to the trade routes than this one, though."

"It sounds ideal. I suggest you slip as soon as possible—it'll be good to get out of this system. I'll have the *Dreamer*'s computer slaved to yours, so when we go through Adverton's system survey to pick out entry coordinates, we won't slip in too far apart. I'd hate to delay our ships' rendezvous."

Ulega Max only looked at me. "What rendezvous? There's no need for delay. We'll go in together. Now."

Shaking my head, I said, "No, I can't agree to that. I still have my cargo to deliver to Duane's World—and you have to find at least one more shuttle . . . not to mention a new captain."

"I'll captain my own ship!"

"You will not," I said sharply. "You know you're not qualified, except in emergencies. Since this one's now over, you must proceed to the nearest planet and hire a new—"

"I'm familiar with League laws!" he snapped. "The Falcon's so automated a rotted bayafruit could pilot her."

"I know." I said, grinning. I could see his temper flaring, but if I let him get away with captaining the *Falcon*, there was no telling where his push for power would stop. "Nevertheless. . . ."

His eyes narrowed. "You'd report us to the Patrol, wouldn't you?"

"That," I said stiffly, "would be my duty, whether I liked it or not."

"I can tell you'd like it. I should've known better than to make a deal with you, Corrian. I made a mistake—"

I was about to return a cutting reply when Vimister Groll made a curt gesture with one withered hand, stopping Max short. "It doesn't matter, Ulega. We'll slip to the nearest major settlement—Verdania, I believe it is—and there we'll hire a new captain. Go on to Duane's World, Kel Corrian. We'll meet you later."

"It's agreed, then." With that, I turned and walked out. I felt Ulega's cold eyes staring at my back until the door shut. Only then did I relax, knowing I'd won everything I'd wanted from them. It was a good deal for both me and my ship.

I let my subordinates on the *Trim Dreamer* work out the details of our deal with Ulega Max, since I didn't particularly want to see him again so soon. We quickly reached an agreeable schedule: after hiring a new captain on Verdania, the *Marrow Falcon* would then proceed on to Adverton and make repairs. By the time I rejoined her, she should be in passable shape, ready to begin processing the hydrogen my ship's shuttles would skim from the star.

It seemed simple enough. But I didn't trust Ulega Max, and I knew that he'd bend the League's laws as much as he dared. And that could prove more dangerous than any star-creatures. The League's laws existed only to protect people from their own foolishness.

Sighing, I leaned back in my seat. I felt suddenly old and tired. It had been a long day. Then Rooli Tebwah called me.

"Yes?" I said.

"Sir, the information's all aboard now."

"Thanks." I turned to Rast, the navigator on duty. "Have you charted the next window to Duane's World?"

"Yes. It'll be at the optimum in a little over three minutes."

Leaning back, I grinned. "That'll be just fine."

I'd already started to think about what to say to Jawn

Kessel. I knew he'd agree with my decision, once I explained everything to him. He had to.

The two of us met in his private quarters early the next day. Jawn Kessel shook his head slowly, as if mystified. "Let me get this straight," he said. "You've agreed to give up our established trade route—which makes enough money for our every need—just to join up with a band of Free Traders who plan to mine stars?"

"Yes."

He sighed. "I must admit I'm rather shocked."

"Sir—please, listen to me. I've seen the jewels they've already made. They may just be synthetics, but they're going to be the next craze to sweep the known universe. No fashionable man or woman will be without them—and they'll pay blood to get them. This was the opportunity of a lifetime. I'd stake my job on it."

"You just did."

I just stared at him, startled and bewildered.

"Kel, profitable trade routes don't just appear. They have to be forged link by link, like a fine gold chain. If the chain breaks, it's because the links weren't strong enough. I spent fifteen years of my life as captain of this ship in all but name. I forged this trade route.

"Still, I do have faith in you. I wouldn't have hired you if you weren't smart and competent. Just see to it my ship makes enough money to keep me happy, all right? I don't want to have to start over again."

"I will, sir." I knew it. This was the chance of a lifetime, and it would make us both rich.

"Slip . . . now."

As the colors shifted up and down the spectrum, I felt a growing sense of disorientation—even Luathek's tinkering with the nullspace power generators hadn't been able to eliminate it. I shook my head, blinked—and we entered the real universe once more.

The trip to Duane's World had been brief. We'd taken orbit around that beautiful blue-green world, unloaded our cargo of ripe bayafruit, waited for payment, and refused to take a shipment of oats and wheat to the ice cities of Frost. The cargo-master hadn't been too disagreeable or hard to handle. He'd even promised us more work, if we ever wanted to start up our trade route again. I'd thanked him warmly.

We slipped out for Adverton the next day.

And, when we entered realspace thirty thousand klicks away from that red dwarf star, heading for our rendezvous with the *Marrow Falcon*—just as I turned to ask Luathek, who stood beside me, for his daily report—

We found ourselves in a battle!

Dazzling streaks of white light flared on the hundreds of video monitors around the room. Alarms began to ring. Several of the more delicate instruments burned out at once, throwing off great showers of sparks. Automatic extinguishers smothered the fires. I was frozen for what seemed an eternity, but it couldn't have been more than a second—my reflexes had always been fast. Even so, Luathek was faster. He leaped into a vacant seat and strapped himself in, manning one of the weapon stations.

The war tact grid had come up the instant our computer noticed the fight going on in the vacuum around us. I slipped inside and tripped all the defense mechanisms—an automatic response that had been drilled into me a thousand times at the Academy. A force shield rose around the *Trim Dreamer*. Her alarm claxons turned to muted, distant, background noise. The control room had been sealed away from the rest of the ship, becoming an isolated world unto itself.

Throughout the *Trim Dreamer*, weapons readied themselves to fire. Hatches slid back in the hull, revealing laser turrets, atomic cannons, a hundred different weapons.

A hologram showed me the situation: fifteen kilometers ahead, the *Marrow Falcon* lay under attack— and her attackers were the star-creatures from Beta Dainis!

At least, I thought so for an instant. Then I noticed differences: these aliens were much smaller, and glowed like paper lanterns with a flame inside. They also seemed to be using some sort of plasma technology—rather than attacking the ship themselves, they held back a good ten kilometers and fired bolt after bolt of sizzling energy. Most trailed off harmlessly into the void, but quite a few struck the *Falcon*'s shields.

In a sudden flash of insight, I realized that there might be star-creatures in every single star throughout the universe! After all, as humanity had spread through the galaxy, we'd found life on almost every world capable of supporting it. If intelligent beings existed in one star, surely they existed in others . . . it was foolish to hope otherwise. Stars were their worlds, and we were invaders. It was a disturbing thought, when looking at things from their point of view. Perhaps that's why they'd attacked the *Falcon*.

The differences between the Advertonian star-creatures and the Beta Dainis star-creatures seemed small on the surface, but I realized they had to be large. I just didn't have the ability to perceive them. (Perhaps all planet-dwellers would look the same to them—cold, hard creatures that crept across cold, hard bits of rock?)

Several of the aliens had turned and begun firing at my ship. From the strain levels registering on the *Trim Dreamer*'s shields, I knew she could hold out against them almost indefinitely. The energy-bolts were all flame and no substance. They couldn't have hurt one of my shuttles . . . or could they?

It was then that I noticed the burned-out wrecks of two small shuttles in the hologram. They floated, lifeless hulks, a scant kilometer from the *Falcon*'s bow. A jolt of shock, anger, and betrayal ran through me—directed not at the star-creatures, but at Ulega Max. He'd betrayed me!

I knew how Ulega Max had gotten the *Falcon* into this situation—he'd ordered the starskimming process to begin without waiting for me. Perhaps he'd planned to manufacture a few extra jewels—jewels which he wouldn't have to share with Jawn Kessel and me.

For a second, I thought about slipping back into nullspace—letting the star-creatures take care of him. After all, he'd provoked them by trying to cheat me. What did I owe him?

Then I sighed. I knew I couldn't just abandon him and his crew. After all, hundreds of people might die. Despite my personal feelings toward him, I couldn't let his innocent crewmen suffer. Plus, I couldn't abandon my investment!

I turned my attention to his ship. The *Falcon*'s shields glowed redly but seemed to be holding—though I couldn't begin to guess how long they'd stand up against the star-creatures' bombardment. Still, if they weren't doing his ship any more harm than they were doing mine, I could well afford to wait and ponder my actions carefully.

What if the star-creatures brought up heavier arms?

I shook my head. No, there would be signs of that.

"Tech Tebwah," I said, "I want to talk to the captain of the *Falcon*. Try and raise him."

"Yes, sir," she said. She turned to the communications console for a moment, then looked back. "Sir, Ulega Max wishes to speak with you."

"I want to speak with the *Falcon*'s captain, not him."

"Captain, he says he is the acting captain."

I cursed and punched him up on my private viewscreen. His scarred face seemed unnaturally serene as he smiled at me. "Ah, Captain Corrian! It's good to see you again."

"I thought you were going to hire a new ship's captain."

"I did." His face hardened. "He died an hour ago, aboard the first shuttle."

"Dying," I said, "seems to be a habit among the captains you hire."

"And to think we almost hired you."

I tried to figure that out—a threat? An insult? A compliment? I couldn't tell. At last, with a dubious shake of my head, I shrugged noncommittally. "Your shields appear to be holding well enough. What do you propose to do?"

"I was just about to set off a round of atomics when you arrived. As our new partner, why don't you take care of it?"

After a moment, I nodded. Perhaps it would be better for me to take care of the matter. He certainly lacked any subtlety.

"I'll handle them," I said coldly.

"Good." His smile was oily. "Do so, then we'll talk." He severed the connection.

I was getting awfully tired of his damned superiority. Leaning back, I thought over my options carefully. It seemed I only had one—attack. How else could I assure the safety of our ships? Still, I knew it would be better if I found my own answer to the problem, rather than obeying him and firing off a round of atomics.

"Kel," Luathek said softly. He'd given up his seat at the weapons station to one of the other officers, then walked to my side while I spoke to Ulega Max.

"Yes, Luathek?"

"The aliens— I know they have intelligences!"

"I can see that. After all, they're using complex weapons."

"No, you are not understanding me. I know it! Their emotions are strong . . . I feel their fear, and anger. They communicate telepathically. They are unlike the other star-creatures we encountered."

"Unlike them— how?"

"I . . . tried to communicate with the others without first informing you. There was so little time, Kel! But I could not reach them. They held themselves apart from me— aloof, as though they wanted no contact between us except death."

I remembered the Pavian's empathic abilities then, remembered how he picked up emotions from those around him. And sometimes, in moments of great stress or fear or need, he managed to pick up thoughts—his empathy turning to true telepathy for a short time. Perhaps, I thought, he'd be able to communicate with the star-creatures, reason with them, work out some sort of trade agreement—

"What about these star-creatures?" I asked. "Will they talk with you? Can you negotiate with them?"

"I am not full of certainty. I think perhaps yes, but it may take some time. They are not trying to shut out my mind, as the others did, which I think is a most favorable sign."

The war tact grid began beeping frantically.

"Wait," I told him. Then I slipped into the grid and studied the computer's projection. It showed a new group of star-creatures leaving Adverton's fringe atmosphere. Streamers of blazing hydrogen trailed out behind them like comet-tails, obscuring their numbers, but I counted at least twenty. Reinforcements? Bringing up stronger weapons?

It didn't take me long to find out. Even before they cleared Adverton, the creatures began shooting at us. And this time, their bolts of energy were a hundred times more powerful—blinding white spheres of pure plasma that came hurtling toward us at nearly the speed of light.

The first one struck the *Marrow Falcon*. It deflected off her force shield, but even that glancing blow set her spinning backwards in a slow end-over-end roll. Slowly, the crew got her stabilized again.

Their second shot sailed past and vanished in the distance—a miss.

The third shot struck my ship. Our shields flickered red and orange as they tried to scatter and diffuse the energy, but that wasn't enough. A bone-jarring shock ran through the hull, strong enough to rattle my teeth. Several viewscreens suddenly showed only static—burned out.

I cursed. In my anger, I almost ordered our atomic cannons to open fire, but caught myself just in time. If we drove them back, then we'd almost certainly never be able to mine this star in peace . . . and yet, if I didn't shoot, both ships might be destroyed at any moment. Did I have time for Luathek to try and communicate with them?

I decided to attack the star creatures. I knew, from my experiences around Beta Dainis, that I could drive them away. That would give us enough time to arrange our next move. *Turn to page 197.*

I decided to try to negotiate. If I can talk to them through Luathek, I might be able to persuade them we weren't an invasion force. We didn't want to fight. *Turn to page 207.*

ON TO DUANE'S WORLD

I shook my head sadly, knowing I'd have to refuse. My responsibility to the *Trim Dreamer* didn't include taking mad gambles with her profits—and this whole starskimming idea seemed like one big risk. A million things could go wrong. How could I give up established trade routes just to chance the unknown? I couldn't. No, it was better for me to take the twenty percent and quit while I was ahead.

"Thanks for the offer," I said reluctantly, thinking once more of those beautiful jewels, "but I have too many other obligations right now."

Ulega Max scowled. "Then leave now. We've told you too much about starskimming already."

"As you wish." Standing, I added, "I'll send you my ship's account number with the League bank. Deposits can be made at your convenience—just so they come regularly."

I knew they'd send me my ship's twenty percent—for all their shortcomings, Free Traders were scrupulously honest. And then I had to remind myself, *if* they make a profit. The whole thing sounded like one mad gamble.

"My assistant is waiting outside," Ulega said. "He can show you the way back to your shuttle."

I bowed stiffly to him. Then, turning, I left.

Jespar Melsif waited outside. He could tell from my expression what had happened, and he tactfully said nothing as he led me toward the lift.

And that was the end of that.

It didn't take long for my techs to get the *Marrow Falcon* operating well enough to make a safe slip to one of the civilized planets. I watched her leave on the viewscreen—first the nullspace power field appeared around her like a veil, then she seemed to shimmer with a thousand different colors, and then—she simply vanished, slipping out of realspace.

I called orders to my crewmen and, in seconds, we too entered nullspace. We continued on to Duane's World and delivered our cargo of bayafruit. From there we went to Zelloque with a shipment of Dozois' Grain, and from there to Pethis, and to Coran, and to Kaldistan—an endless cycle through the same solar systems, carrying the same cargoes time and time again.

I often wondered what happened to the *Marrow Falcon*. Then, after six months of silence, we received a payment, then another. Soon we were getting fifty to seventy-five thousand royals roughly every other month—huge sums, to a marginally profitable trade ship like the *Dreamer*. The money put us firmly in the black, allowing Jawn Kessel to pay for numerous small improvements throughout the ship. The engines were recalibrated, the repeller fields fine-tuned, the computers updated.

Then, on holos, I started seeing newscasts which mentioned a new jewel-craze sweeping among the nobly born throughout the universe. I knew, then, that Ulega Max had managed to find an uninhabited star to skim.

As I lay awake at nights, I thought of the offer he'd made—fifty percent of his ship's earnings. It would've been a fortune, enough for me to buy my own ship out of my share, enough for me to set myself up for life.

Perhaps I'd been a fool to pass up the opportunity. Perhaps—

I shook my head slowly. No, I'd made the right decision for me. I might not get rich running the *Dreamer*'s trade route, but I'd never starve, either. She was a good ship, with a good crew, and I was satisfied with that.

And yet . . . I couldn't help but wonder what I might've accomplished if I'd only had the courage to join up with the Free Traders. The thought haunted me.

What if . . .

THE END

DEATH OF A STARSHIP

I decided to attack. After all, they'd started the fight—and I didn't want to take any chances with my ship or crew. I didn't have time to let Luathek try and talk to them—things were happening too fast. If more of those plasma balls struck our shields. . . . I didn't want to think about it.

"Kel?" Luathek said. "Should I try to talk to the aliens?"

I shook my head. "No. We'll drive them back first, then see what we can do to communicate with them. Take one of the empty weapons stations."

"Yes, Kel. As you say." He turned and went back to a console, then strapped himself into the chair.

The other techs began calling their targets, zeroing in on the star-creatures with both lasers and atomic missiles.

I slipped back into the war tact grid. Images appeared before me, the twenty new star-creatures had just about reached the first group. Flashing green markers showed which ones had been targeted by my gunners. I was just about to order the attack to begin when several star-creatures fired again, and three glowing white balls of energy hurtled toward the *Marrow Falcon*.

They struck one after another in quick succession—and a brilliant red-white light flared around the other ship. For an instant, I thought the *Falcon* had been vaporized, but then I saw her glide safely through the inferno. Her shields had held after all. I'd been gripping the arms of my seat with painful strength and forced myself to let go.

And then the *Falcon*'s force shields went down. Bright sparks and sheets of electricity leaped across her hull. She trembled, as if rocked by internal explosions, and I cursed helplessly under my breath as I watched her. There was nothing I could do now—except prevent the star-creatures from finishing her off.

The last of the target-markers appeared on my war tact screen. The lights blinked *Ready.* "Fire!" I shouted.

At once lasers fired from their turrets, lancing the darkness, striking the aliens—but with no apparent effect. Then fifteen missiles leaped from my ship's cannons, a round of atomics powerful enough to utterly destroy a good-sized city on any planet.

The star-creatures managed to fire one last ball of plasma energy. I watched as my missiles streaked across the screen, entered the massed crowd of star-creatures, and detonated. Huge rings of white light spread out, their centers marking the spots where they'd exploded. I held my breath, tension jangling my nerves, as the glow slowly faded.

Only then could the war tact grid pick up the star-creatures again. And they were retreating! They almost broke the light barrier in their haste to make it back to Adverton and safety. We'd won!

Around me, my crew cheered.

I slipped from the computer screen. Then I remembered Ulega Max and the *Marrow Falcon*—what had happened to them? I slipped back into the war tact grid . . . and gaped in shock.

The star-creatures' last shot had been their most devastating. A huge hole gaped in the middle of the *Falcon's* hull. It went completely through the ship, only a few thin strands of metal held the bow and stern halves together. The *Trim Dreamer* could've passed through the hole without touching either side. I had a bad feeling in the pit of my stomach as I slipped from the computer screen and turned to my communications officer.

"Tech Tebwah," I said, "I want to speak with Ulega Max again."

"Aye, Captain." She turned to her communications equipment and, within ten seconds, had raised the Free Trader ship.

Ulega Max's face appeared on my chair's viewscreen. There was a cut on his forehead. Blood ran down his face. From what I could see of the chamber behind him, I knew the star-creatures hadn't damaged that part of the *Falcon*—but then, the control room was the most secure area on any ship. Still, they had to have felt the force of that last strike—it must've tossed them around the room like paper toys in a wind tunnel. Ulega seemed to be in a mild shock. He just stared at me without recognition.

"Ulega Max," I said, "what's the status of your ship?"

He didn't seem to hear.

"Captain Ulega Max—tell me the status of your ship!" I put as much authority behind my voice as I could.

It seemed to work. He began to respond. His eyes moved down to the controls before him and he mumbled, "Two compartments plus the control room still intact. Survivors . . . there are thirty-nine of us here . . . nobody left alive besides us. Nullspace power fields can't be generated. No thrusters. Emergency batteries will last another eight hours." He looked up at me. "We're a floating hulk. The ship's a total loss."

"No, it isn't," I said crisply. "Your control room can be separated from the ship—launched as a shuttle, if it's still intact. Check and see."

He turned and spoke with some of the techs behind him. They nodded and said something back—I couldn't hear what. Finally he turned back to me and said, "The control room's intact. I hadn't realized there were emergency power generators here."

"That," I said, "is why you weren't qualified to be the *Marrow Falcon*'s captain."

"What should I do now?" he asked. He looked at me for help. All the pent-up anger and hostility in him was gone. He was a mere a shell of his former self, weak and empty, somehow pitiful. "What should I do now?"

"Finish up everything you need to do, then free the control room and launch it. You can dock with my ship—there's an empty shuttle bay—and then we'll talk about our next move."

Slowly, he nodded. I reached out and shut off the viewscreen.

Time passed slowly. The destruction of the *Marrow Falcon* cast a pall over everything. Everyone aboard my ship felt it—a deep sense of loss. Death is a very personal thing in space, where any error can cost a man his life, or a ship its existence. Almost two hundred people dead . . . it was quite a blow. I wondered, then, if any of the Ship's Council had survived, besides Ulega Max. Vimister Groll had struck me as a survivor. I knew deep inside that he still lived—that he'd soon be aboard my ship, enjoying my and Jawn Kessel's hospitality. I knew it.

"Captain," Rast said, from his navigator's station.

"Hmm? What is it?"

"They've launched their control room. I've already fed their navcomputer the proper course. They'll be docking here within half an hour."

I nodded. "Good. And, while they're doing that, you can prepare to launch one of our shuttles. After Ulega Max and his men dock, you can stake our claim to the *Falcon*."

He just looked at me, puzzled. "Sir?"

"It's salvage." I smiled. "Since they abandoned her, she's fair game for the first to post notice. And that's going to be us." And I thought, since I had to give up the *Trim Dreamer*'s trade route because of them, it's only fair that we take payment for our lost earnings.

"Yes, sir." He stood and went to the lift, then headed down toward the shuttle bays.

When I went to meet Ulega Max and the rest of the *Falcon*'s survivors, I was hardly prepared for the procession that passed through the airlock. First came Ulega Max—his head now bandaged, wearing a clean gray uniform—followed by Vimister Groll and Yamal Hydrif. A dozen white-uniformed techs walked through next—scientists? After them came various guards and the techs who'd been on duty in the control room at the time of the attack.

Ulega Max, it seemed, had managed to save all the most valuable members of his crew. I guessed the men and women in white were the ones who ran the equipment that manufactured super-heated hydrogen into jewels . . . the people he'd need to start processing again. Had Ulega somehow known the *Falcon* would be destroyed—and taken steps to keep their livelihood going? No . . . it couldn't be that. Somehow he'd just been fortunate with the ship's survivors. Ghu knew he hadn't been lucky with anything else.

Smiling, I bowed cordially to the Ship's Council. "I'm pleased to find you all still alive."

"No more so than me," Vimister Groll said. "It's a good thing I always prepare for emergencies. Our loss is enormous, though."

"The ship. . . ."

"Eh? More than the ship. I lost my whole collection of old Earth vids! They were priceless." There was real grief in his voice.

"Perhaps they can be salvaged."

"No. They were fragile things; open vaccuum will have completely destroyed them."

I shrugged. He was a crazy old man to be worrying about old vidtapes, when his entire ship—his entire life— had just been destroyed. Free Traders, I thought. I'd never understand them.

"Accommodations have been made for your stay here. There are enough free cabins for you and your crew— although some of your people will have to double-up. I trust the inconvenience won't bother them?"

"It won't," Ulega Max said. His lips were pressed in a tight line. Free Traders hated charity. "Now, if you can make arrangements to bring us to the nearest spaceport, we need to secure another ship as soon as possible."

"Certainly," I said. "Just as soon as my men are finished with the *Falcon*."

He started. "What do you mean, 'finished with the *Falcon*'?"

"Simply that. Now that you've launched the control room and officially abandoned her, she's salvage. One of my officers has already gone over to stake our claim to her. Everything aboard is mine now. Of course, you'll get your ten percent of the value, just as League law stipulates." I turned toward the lift. "Now, if you'll follow me, I'll bring you down to the spare cabins."

"You can't do that!" Max was practically frothing at the mouth.

"I can," I said grimly. "It's my insurance policy about our partnership. We'll talk about it later tonight, after supper. Now I have other, more pressing things to take care of—like getting you settled. Follow me."

I started for the lift and, damned if Max didn't grab my arm! I jerked free, then turned to face him. His face was red with shock and anger and he was shouting, "You're a pirate, Corrian! We didn't abandon our ship. You invited us here—you know that!"

I frowned. "I don't like your attitude, Captain Max. Need I remind you that you're a guest on my ship? If you wanted to keep control of the *Falcon*, you should've left people aboard her. The League is quite clear about that."

"I didn't know—"

"The League's laws cover that, too. Ignorance is no excuse. A trained captain would have known." I shrugged. "Or, the information was available to you—from your ship's computer."

He said nothing. I looked at Vimister Groll, who only nodded. "We ask your forgiveness, Captain Corrian," he said. "The loss of the ship is . . . upsetting to all of us."

I bowed my head. "As you say." Then I turned and entered the lift, careful not to give Ulega another chance to protest.

He had no choice but to follow.

The *Falcon*'s Ship's Council met with Jawn Kessel and me in a small, comfortable conference room later that night. I'd cautioned the *Trim Dreamer*'s owner to let me negotiate. I knew how far I could push Ulega Max and Vimister Groll, and I knew what sort of deal I could get from them if everything went as well as I hoped it would.

I cleared my throat. "Let's be brief," I said. "Whether you like it or not, I'm going to take all the starskimming equipment from what's left of your ship and install it here."

"You'll never figure out how to use it," Ulega Max said sharply, "and even if you do, you don't have the specialists to run the machinery. We're not worried about competition from the likes of you."

I shrugged. "The universe is large, with lots of stars. Even if star-creatures are as common as they appear to be, surely we'll still be able to find plenty of uninhabited suns to skim. Even if we were both manufacturing jewels, there wouldn't be any problem."

"You seem to know exactly what you want," Ulega said, a note of bitterness creeping into his voice. "What's that got to do with us?"

"Quite a lot. You've been through numerous shocks lately. Perhaps you haven't realized that the best possible thing to do would be to keep our partnership going."

"Never!"

Vimister Groll glared at him. "Ulega . . . we have discussed this."

"You were wrong—let me handle it my way."

"No. If you speak for the Council, you must abide by our decisions."

I stared at the two of them, unsure of what to say or do next. There seemed to be a major disagreement between Ulega and the rest of the *Falcon's* Ship's Council.

As last Ulega sat down and looked at the far wall. "Then I will not speak for the Council."

Vimister Gross pursed his lips, then turned to me and Jawn Kessel. "Forgive the unpleasantness, good sirs. We're quite willing to listen to your suggestions. What, exactly, do you propose?"

"Quite simply this: We have a ship and three shuttles. We'll soon have the processing equipment on board. You have the techs necessary to run the equipment. It seems obvious that a greater partnership is in order. I'm no longer the unnecessary intruder who has forced himself into the deal. You need me now. I want to continue the partnership."

Vimister Groll hesitated.

I pressed my point. "If you buy a new ship now, it's either going to be much smaller than you want, or it'll push you so far into debt you'll be paying the interest for the next twenty years. However, if we begin starskimming within the month—and have the first jewels on the market within six months from now—your share of the profit would give you more than enough to re-equip."

"And what do you get out of it?" Vimister Groll asked shrewdly.

"We get, first of all, half the profits. And you'll see that my crew is trained to use the starskimming equipment. When you have your own ship, I don't expect you to stay around and help me run the *Trim Dreamer*."

"That would make us trade rivals!"

I shook my head. "Partners. Anyhow, that's a year away. And besides, the demand for the jewels will be so great, we won't have to under-cut each other. We can keep prices as high as we want."

The three Ship's Councilmen exchanged glances, then nodded.

"Very well," Vimister Groll said. "We accept the deal— for now."

"Good." I nodded enthusiastically. "I already have papers drawn up and ready to sign. . . ."

"Wait," Ulega said sharply. "Since we're going to be partners *again,* I insist we reach some sort of understanding."

"About what?" I said.

"Salvaging the ship. Forcing our techs to train yours. Everything."

"I see what you mean," I said.

"Do you?" He sneered. "Partners don't take advantage of one another's weaknesses."

"And they don't sneak around and begin skimming Adverton without waiting for the other ship to arrive," I returned coldly. Ulega's face paled when I mentioned that.

Apparently, he'd forgotten how he'd lost his ship in the first place. "The minute you did that, our original partnership ended. Therefore I feel no guilt about trying to make a better deal this time—one which you won't be able to get out of so easily."

Dead silence. Then Vimister Groll began to laugh.

"That," he said, "is true. You have a bargain, Kel Corrian—and partners once more."

"Good." And we shook hands to seal the deal.

Jawn Kessel was looking at me admiringly. As Ship's Owner, he'd make a fortune from this. But my share of the profits wouldn't be too bad! Already, I was thinking ahead. We'd finish the salvage work here as quickly as possible, then move on. Find a star that wasn't inhabited this time. And we'd make our profits, and soon I'd quit as the *Trim Dreamer*'s captain and buy my own vessel—and skim my own stars. I intended to learn every detail of the starskimming process.

I'd be a rich man when I retired. I knew it as surely as I'd known Ulega Max, Vimister Groll, and Yamal Hydrif would agree to my partnership.

I smiled.

THE END

MESSIAH

I decided to try to negotiate with the creatures—after all, I didn't want to fight a war with them! If possible, I wanted their help. They'd make the best possible allies, since they could move through their star's atmosphere at will.

They fired another bolt of energy. It missed the *Falcon*—barely.

"Luathek," I said, slipping from the war tact grid, "talk to them. You've got to tell them not to shoot at us!"

He nodded. "Yes, Kel. Immediately." A passive expression came over his face as he turned his thoughts inward, seeking whatever mental controls he used. His eyestalks coiled like snakes among the gray tufts of hair on his head.

I re-entered the war tact grid. The star-creatures seemed about to fire their weapons again, but for some reason they stopped before doing so. With a sigh of relief I leaned back, certain that Luathek had, somehow, managed to reach them.

The Pavian showed no sign of returning to this world. His breath came slowly and regularly, and his face remained unreadable. What was he telling them? Would they listen?

Suddenly his eyes opened. He gasped, his expression one of shock and pain rather than pleasure.

"Luathek— ?" I began.

He looked at me. His eyes were strangely dark. "AhhhKeh-h-h—"

"What is it?" I whispered. I could almost feel the struggle going on inside him, as though he were battling the creatures for control of his body.

"Kel," he said, quite distinctly. Then: "I—am most—sorry!"

And something hard and heavy hit me straight between the eyes with the force of a falling meteor.

I felt a quick flash of excruciating pain, then a numbness came over me. My head was a cold lump. I couldn't feel my arms or legs—couldn't move—

Slowly, awareness of a sort returned. I saw myself walking down an endless white corridor. Somewhere ahead, I knew, Luathek waited for me. I could hear his voice calling from a great distance.

I walked for what seemed an eternity. The corridor's glowing white walls became more distinct, as my mind focused on them, made them real. And then I heard Luathek's voice clearly.

Open your mind to me, Kel.

For the longest time I just stood there, bewildered, unable to make sense of the words. They seemed to be in some alien tongue. I couldn't associate them with any pictures or actions.

Kel. . . . Luathek. I knew it was him. Shaking my head, I tried to shrug off the lethargy that had settled over my mind and began to run.

The Pavian appeared in front of me, suddenly, hovering a foot above the floor, his arms outspread in a gesture of welcome or submission. Again he called my name, and this time the meaning of his words reached me.

I closed my eyes and let his thoughts become mine.

A roar filled my head, the sound of rushing waves on an Earth beach. A strange feeling of power swept through my body. The endless white corridor melted away and I could see nothing ahead but the textured blackness of space—scattered with pinpricks of light that could only be distant stars—and yet I knew this was but another phantasm conjured up by Luathek's powerful mind.

Here I would meet the star-creatures.

A sound called to me. At first I thought it was a voice, then I realized that within it echoed not words, but emotions . . . dizzying waves of fear and apprehension, peaks of red anger and hatred and pain. For an instant, the universe swung crazily around and I looked through alien eyes, felt alien thoughts—and saw myself differently.

It was as if an inanimate object—something too massive to possibly move, to possibly live—wavered there before me. How could something with such densely packed molecules possibly live? How could it flow from one place to another? What made it think? Surely its mindbody could not be the same as ours?

Then I drifted apart from the awareness—and I knew. *I* was the strange creature with densely packed molecules! And then I wondered how I could move from one place to another—it seemed so impossible . . .

Kel, a distant voice intruded. *I can feel their presences.*

Luathek? I thought.

Talk to them, Kel—I may not be able to hold them in my mind much longer than this.

I tried to reach out a second time—to hear their thoughts and make them hear mine. An odd, tingling sensation filled my mind, somehow blanking out my every will to move. It was as though I'd lost control of all voluntary muscles. I'd become an observer, locked in my body, looking out on a world I couldn't control. I hated and feared this feeling of helplessness more than anything else.

And then I realized the star-creatures had become aware of me. My perceptions took a sudden leap outward and I knew what had happened—their minds had reached through Luathek and entered my body.

And I'd let them do it.

———

I had none of the Pavian's mental training. On Pavo IV, his homeworld, the young were taught to master whatever telepathic and empathic powers lay within them almost from the minute of their hatching. He had discipline where I had nothing but raw instinct. My brain might short-circuit under the star-creatures' heavy-handed prodding.

And I felt them sorting through my mind.

Now images flew uncontrolled before my eyes: my mother and father, life on my homeworld of Bernstrom's algae farms, the League's teaching machines and ability-tests, my appointment to the Academy on a scholarship, my apprenticeship to Yer Makov in space, all the planets I'd visited, all the starships I'd worked on.

And Luathek, Versachio Grel, Ulega Max, everyone else I'd ever known. All my memories came and went faster than I could think of them—sucked out of my mind. All the pettiness, all the pain, all the love and generosity, all the flaws and all the beauty that make life worth living—it all passed through Luathek and entered the minds of the star-creatures.

If it had been possible, I would have wept. My insides seethed with memories of anger and passion. A great desire burned within me—to return to all the places of my youth, to recapture old loves and settle old grudges. People I hadn't seen in decades haunted me. I couldn't think. All I could do was hold my feelings back, try and regain control over all my past lives as they rushed past.

And still the star-creatures probed at me. I saw them now, a dozen beings like drops of silver hanging in the nighttime sky. They pushed and pulled at my memories, rummaging through them as though they were old clothes, stealing them.

I stood at the edge of the algae fields, looking out across the hectares of shallow lakes filled with gray-green slime.

Harvesters waded across the fields, their three long, thin legs dipping into the water with giant scoops. My father stood behind me, his hand on my shoulder.

"See there," he said, pointing. "That flash of silver? That's an alien. Somehow it got down here and now it's living off the algae. Now watch the harvesters there. Those three are going to try to kill it."

And, within me, I felt a deepening sense of horror and sadness. I almost cheered when the silver flash in the water darted out of sight, escaping the harvesters—this time.

I was in the nullspace simulation chamber of the Academy, sitting in a captain's seat, locked in one of the computer's navigation screens. A red alarm-light flashed in the screen's upper right corner.

"Hull breached, Captain," the computer's soft voice said in my ear. "I request instructions."

And I didn't know what to do—didn't know—

The red light stopped flashing. The navigation screen collapsed, and I looked out on Instructor Roland's unsmiling face. Her black uniform with the gold bars of her rank was immaculate. She demanded perfection, even of herself. Panic rushed through me. I began to tremble.

"You're dead now, Corrian," she said. "What's even worse, you also killed one hundred and eight crew members. They're all dead because you panicked. Dead, Corrian, one hundred and eight people dead because you didn't listen to my instructions."

"But they weren't real!"

"They were real. You'll never gain rank until you can see even the slightest possibility of danger to your crew as real, Corrian."

I bit my lip and couldn't speak and—

This time it was different—I felt it. My body was thick and heavy, as though I waded through an ocean of molasses. I turned to speak to Luathek, who walked beside me, but as I did so, he started to turn transparent. By the time I'd recovered from my surprise, he'd completely disappeared.

My mind seemed to be fragmenting. Snatches of conversations I couldn't possibly be hearing came to me. I thought thoughts that were human but not my own, and I saw sights through human eyes that I couldn't possibly be seeing.

I was *two* people in the weapons room, talking about the star-creatures—I was both of them at once, seeing each side of the conversation, knowing what each man would say before he opened his mouth.

I was alone in one of the shuttles, thinking, What if Corrian sends me out there to fight them?

I was at the communications station (Rooli Tebwah?) thinking, Kel knows what he's doing. He won't let us die.

And there were a hundred others, all different, all calling for my attention. I was Vimister Groll, and Ulega Max, and Jespar Melsif, and all the others on the *Falcon*. I was Luathek and Rast and Jawn Kessel and everyone on the *Trim Dreamer*. Their voices clawed at my mind. I could scarcely think—

But by now the universe around me had disappeared. I floated in an absolute void, lost, without sense of right or left or up or down. I fell in all directions at once.

I couldn't even hear myself screaming.

The world reconstitutes itself around me.

I am at Gwinney's Circus.

Sounds drift through the summer cold, oozing across the grass as a blue and purple tide. The Old Earth elephants are dancing above me on the high-wire. . . . Distorted memories: I recall seeing huge circuses on vidtapes, and a small one with a fascinating freak show on New Swanwick. But I know they weren't like this. This is so . . . unreal, weaving in and out of the billowing red odors of animals. I crack my whip and watch the sharp yellow sound move steadily upwards.

Ulega Max dances to my side.

"Would you like to play a game of Moopsball?" he asks. The words are pale bubbles that brush my skin and send shivers up my spine.

The circus shimmers and falls away, leaving us on a gigantic Moopsball field—almost a full square hectare of barren, featureless, orange land. Two small pavillions, with red pennants on top, sit to my far right and left, and before them float gigantic disks of bronze.

Hundreds of oddly dressed humans wander the playing field, their movements apparently aimless, random. I recognize dozens of them from the *Trim Dreamer* . . . and others from the *Marrow Falcon*—over there Vimister Groll, over here Ulega Max and Jespar Melsif—

A dozen suns burn overhead. On each can be seen a single giantic eye. They are our masters, I know. They will judge the game. It has always been this way . . . and I have the feeling that this game has been played out many times before, with humans as giant puppets and event following event in an endless, meaningless cycle.

Trumpets sound. Their notes are mournful.

The lancers have taken up their arms and mounted their giant pink war-elephants. They charge across the battlefield, hooves thundering. Then the elephants on one side shimmer and change to sleek black starships, and the elephants on the other become flaming yellow stars.

Lights flare. In an instant all the starships explode, sending little bits of twisted, melted metal spinning off in all directions. And all the humans inside writhe and scream in pain, the awful sound of their cries ringing end-lessly in my ears.

A message? That we should leave this star—or we'd be killed? I think that is what the vision means.

And the crewmen die, and I watch them die, and I'm powerless to stop what's happening. But I feel their pain as intensely as I've ever felt anything before. It becomes my own, and through me their suffering is eased.

I look down at my hands. They are badly burned, blood drips from the tips of my fingers, spatters on the ground at my feet, loses itself in the orange soil. Raising my arms to the suns overhead, I let the watchers see my wounds. In a sudden hot glow of light, I am healed.

The crewmen from both ships crowd around me. There is reverence in their manner, and a sense of awe is evident on their faces. They raise their arms to me, and a hundred voices cry my name, and the name of their god:

"Kel! Kel!"

"Ghu! Ghu!"

I look at them, and it is with a strange sense of dread and foreboding that I turn to run. But they are all around me, and their hands reach out to guide my course so I move deeper into the mob, rather than away. I am their center, and a vortex forms around me.

Above, the brilliantly shining suns leave one by one, comet-tails streaming out behind them. They flow higher, grow smaller in the distance, soon vanish completely from view. Darkness like velvet fills the heavens. My people and I are alone now—we will remain that way, so long as we leave the star-creatures and their . . . world? . . . untouched. I know it more surely than I have ever known anything before. Their message has reached me.

The crewmen are all around me now, clustering like sheep, reaching out to touch my clothes. They seize my

---

arms and legs and raise me into the air and I am screaming and the sky overhead is spinning round and round and—

I opened my eyes and found myself back aboard the *Trim Dreamer*, in the captain's seat in the control room. My head ached. I could feel my heart pounding in my chest, a wild, alien rhythm. I closed my eyes and made my heart's beating slow to a more normal speed. The Academy's courses in yoga and mental conditioning had their uses . . . I only wished they'd taught psychic disciplines as well.

"Luathek," I whispered.

The Pavian stood motionless near my chair, his face pale, his gaze lost in the distance. Slowly, as if responding to his name, he turned and looked up at me. Expression came into his eyes. His eyestalks writhed happily as he showed rows of sharp black teeth in an approximation of a smile.

"Kel," he said, "I could talk with them—they will let us leave in peace! Did you hear them? I tried to let you communicate through me—that is what they wished—but. . . ." His voice trailed off. He glanced around the room. "Why is everyone observing you thusly, Kel?" he asked.

"What?" I followed his gaze. Everyone had turned to stare at me, mingled joy and bewilderment on their faces.

Rooli Tebwah said softly, "Ghu's new messiah has come at last!"

"Don't be ridiculous," I snapped. "Get on with your work. I don't have time for such nonsense."

"Sir . . . I felt it! We all felt it. It came as a great vision. You stood before us, taking away all the pain of the universe. I saw it!"

A dozen voices echoed her words. They all left their posts and crowded around my chair, kneeling down before me, reaching out to touch the hem of my trousers—

"Master, what must we do?" Rooli asked. "Master?" They'd all shared my hallucinations, I realized suddenly. The visions the star-creatures used to order me away from their star had affected them, too. Only they hadn't understood, the message hadn't been directed at them, but at me. And now they believed I was some sort of . . . messiah?

"Get back to your posts," I said, a bit shakily.

They did so—instantly. And then they began to sing.

The words weren't in Basic, but in an older human tongue—English, which the Free Traders used for their religious ceremonies. It was a strange, guttural language, with odd inflections and long, rising vowels. I shivered as they sang, for somehow they'd added my name into the song.

I'd been born of groundirt parents, not of Free Trader stock, and I'd never understood them and their strange ways. I'd always been an outsider into the mysteries of their faith, for none but those of Trader blood could ever take part in their religious ceremonies.

"Stop it!" I shouted. "Don't sing—and don't think of me as your messiah, because I'm not!"

"Yes, Kel Corrian," Rooli said. But I could tell she hadn't truly heard what I'd said.

I rose to my feet, my legs strangely weak. I staggered. A dozen people leaped up and surged forward to help me, but I swung a fist at them and cursed, so they backed away. Still, they seemed determined to make me into their messiah.

And I wondered, then, whether I shouldn't just go along with them and let them make me into a god. Throughout history, people had done just that to found new religions. And those messiahs had lived in splendor, with thousands—hundreds of thousands—of servants at their beck and call. I could see it now: my followers from the *Trim Dreamer* and the *Marrow Falcon* sweeping across the universe, spreading word of their visions to all the Free Traders.

And they'd come to me, I knew, from all corners of the known universe, bringing offerings of gold and jewels and whatever else I wanted. They could carve out a vast trade empire, make me one of the most powerful people in the League. . . .

But, even as I thought of it, I knew I'd never let it happen. I had no desire for the life of an absolute monarch. I wanted to travel, to see the universe, to be—myself. I'd always been scrupulously honest in all my dealings, and the thought of lying to millions of Free Traders, of saying I was the voice of their god, made me uneasy to say the least.

I knew I'd never be able to go through with such a scheme.

Turning, I fled to the lift. I needed time to think. Behind me, the singing started again, and I could hear Rooli Tebwah's high, clear voice above all the rest. Shaken, I punched the button and the doors closed. I headed down, toward the lower decks and my cabin.

It was with a measure of anger and frustration that I finally emerged from my room three hours later. I'd thought it all over and believed I had an answer to my problem—a way to prove I wasn't their messiah. All I had to do was demonstrate my lack of Ghu-given powers—and I counted on Ulega Max for help. He wasn't the gullible sort. He had to think I'd somehow faked the visions.

But they were waiting for me in the hallway. Twenty people custered around me, trying to beg favors, trying to get miracles worked. Jawn Kessel was among them—and he seemed as believing as the rest.

I shouted until they all grew quiet. Their eyes were very round and very large.

"I must go to the *Marrow Falcon*," I said. "Prepare my shuttle. The rest of you can help me, too."

"How?" they called. "Tell us, Master!"

"By returning to your posts. By performing your duties as if nothing had changed—at least for now. There will be important work for you later. Trust me."

And they did. They all turned and ran off, leaving me there alone. More slowly now, I walked toward the shuttle bay. I knew the *Trim Screamer* would be ready for take-off by the time I arrived.

The situation was much the same aboard the *Marrow Falcon*. I received docking clearance and a request for a minor miracle—for me to cure deafness in the communications officer's left ear. Pointedly ignoring her, I had my shuttle's pilot dock.

I'd passed through the airlock almost before the engines shut down.

A multitude waited for me in the loading bay. There must've been over a hundred of them—men and women, a sprinking of humanoid aliens, most of the *Falcon*'s crew. They knelt before me and shouted my name over and over again, an endless chant:

"Kel! Kel! Kel!"

I held up my hands, and they grew silent. Leaning forward, they strained to hear my every word. And I didn't disappoint them.

"Citizens," I said, "you have been chosen for a very important task. I will speak to each of you personally later today. Important things must be done. But first you must keep this ship running smoothly. It's important to my cause. Go about your work, and rejoice, for you serve Ghu well. Now return to your posts."

They rose to their feet and filed toward the exits. Someone began to sing—the same English song that I'd heard on the *Trim Dreamer*.

I followed them, patting some on the back, whispering encouraging words to others. Nowhere in the crowd did I spot the members of the Ship's Council. I guessed they were in some sort of emergency meeting.

Then I turned around and found myself standing toe to toe with Ulega Max. He glared at me, but said nothing until all the faithful had gone and we were alone. His voice echoed loudly in the loading bay as he said,

"I don't know how you did it, Corrian, but I don't like it." His eyes narrowed. "I want you to stay out of my mind—and off of my ship."

"Listen to me," I said. "It was all an accident. I never meant for any of this to happen. "I . . . tried to negotiate with the star-creatures."

He snorted.

"It's true," I said. "Luathek, the Pavian you met earlier, is empathic—and, to some small extent, telepathic. He served as a bridge between me and the aliens. Unfortunately, it seems that some of that telepathic communication spilled over into the minds of everyone around me—including both ships' crews. They're convinced I'm some sort of messiah sent from Ghu, and I haven't been able to convince them otherwise."

"I . . . almost believed it myself," Ulega Max admitted, still watching me suspiciously. "Then I looked at you and knew no god worth his weight in air could possibly choose you to be his messiah. I've never believed that superstitious rot about Ghu and Fufu and their cosmic war, anyway. It's just old tales meant to frighten children."

"Nothing more?"

"Nothing." He shook his head. "Nothing."

I sighed in relief. Good old cynical Max! "Then you'll help me stop them?"

"Of course!" He smiled broadly, the first time I'd seen him do so. "Come, we've got to go to your cabin. I'll tell you my plan on the way."

It began easily enough. We simply let one of his shuttle Commanders—her name was Omm and she carried herself with authority—into the audience chamber just outside Ulega's private quarters. At first sight, she fell to her knees before me and made some sort of religious gestures with her right hand while she clutched a gold double-helix medallion with her left.

"Get up," I told her.

She did so, looking happier than any Free Trader I'd ever seen before, just from obeying my simple request.

Then I said, as bluntly as I could, "I want you to go into the nearest airlock and throw yourself into space."

She blinked. "Master?"

"You heard me. Go space yourself. I've decided I want your job. And, of course, I'll take all your money as well. I'm going to go to Duane's World and buy myself a luxury house. I hear there's good money in hydro-farming these days. There's probably enough royals on this ship to set me up for life."

She was staring at me wildly. "But . . . you're supposed to put aside all thoughts of worldy goods. You're supposed to help me make my life better, not order me to kill myself!"

I shrugged. "What do I care what happens to you, so long as I get your money? That's all I want."

She stammered helplessly for a minute. Then her face grew hard. "If that's all you want, you won't have it from me. You're no messiah!" She started forward, raising her fists, but Ulega Max grabbed her arms and forced them down.

"Be quiet, Commander Omm," he said. "Of course Corrian isn't a messiah. The vision you thought you had was just telepathy. Nothing more. He's just a man. And what he did now was for your own good—you must believe that."

"But," she whispered, "what if I'd really killed myself?"

"We wouldn't have let that happen, would we, Corrian?"

I shook my head. "Certainly not."

She sighed, and a wistful expression appeared on her face for just an instant. I knew what she was thinking. She was imagining everything that might have been possible if only I had, in fact, been their messiah. At last she sighed and straightened up, asking,

"What can I do to help?"

I grinned at her. "Just try and keep your crewmates from hitting me when I tell them all I want is their money."

Ulega Max was already at the door, showing the next believer in. This one was a heavy-set guard—and he wore a blaster strapped to his right leg.

"Uh," I said, as he knelt before me. "May I see that weapon, please?"

He handed it to me with a sort of awe. Smiling, I tucked it into my sash. And then I told him to space himself . . . and watched his expression turn from reverence to instant hate. He leaped for my throat, but Commander Omm got to him first and pinned him to the floor, neatly and efficiently. She was a good officer.

Ulega Max began explaining everything to the guard.

From here on, I knew, it would be easy.

———

It took the rest of the day to convince everyone on board the *Falcon* that I wasn't a messiah, that they hadn't had a mystical vision, and that nothing had changed for them or the universe. A bit to my surprise, not one of the Free Traders agreed to go kill himself. I would've thought there'd be at least one fanatic on board . . . but perhaps not.

Then we moved to the *Trim Dreamer* and finished there in a little under two hours. I'd had Ulega Max and Commander Omm with me the whole time, and after drinks and a suitable display of thanks on both our parts, I escorted them to my shuttle, the *Trim Screamer.*

As he headed into the airlock, Ulega turned to me. There was a thoughtful expression on his face. "Corrian," he said, "I didn't think I'd like you when we first met. I hated you when you refused the captainship I offered. Now . . . I feel a certain respect for you. I think the partnership between our vessels will work out after all."

"We'll move on to another star," I said. "One that isn't inhabited. There's profit enough in those jewels for both of us."

"Perhaps," he said. Then he turned and followed Commander Omm into the airlock. It cycled and he was gone.

I had a good feeling inside. I'd never thought to see the day when a high Free Trader official would ever acknowledge respect for me. It wasn't their way.

With a light heart, I headed toward the control room. My crew had been suitably embarassed by the whole affair, and I had to show them it didn't matter—that everything would soon be back to normal.

I'd see to that, like any good captain.

THE END

———

ABOUT THE AUTHOR

John Gregory Betancourt was born in Missouri. He moved to New Jersey early in life and resides there currently. Besides writing short stories for fantasy and science fiction magazines, John is assistant editor of AMAZING® STORIES magazine, and writes a book review column for that publication. STARSKIMMER is his first science fiction novel. He has recently sold his first fantasy novel—THE BLIND ARCHER—to Avon.